Todd turned to Elizabeth, and she cringed at the look of disbelief on his face. She'd never seen Todd so upset. "Why would you let Devon believe Jessica was you?"

"You don't understand," Elizabeth choked out. "I didn't want to hurt—"

"I'll tell you why," Devon snapped, his hands balling into fists. "Because sweet little Elizabeth wanted to lead us both on."

A small crowd had formed, but Elizabeth ignored them, her heart aching as she struggled to find a way out of the mess she and Jessica had created. But Todd's face suddenly lost all its color, and he turned to her again, his expression totally heartbroken. His voice sounded hoarse when he spoke. "Liz, tell me it's not true. Please, tell me . . . it's not true."

Elizabeth choked on a sob. She covered her mouth, her body trembling. How could she tell Todd the truth when she didn't know what it was anymore—when she was in love with both of them, but she'd hurt them both? She looked at Devon's angry, unforgiving face, then back at Todd's devastated expression, and she realized she didn't have the words. The tension raced between them, charged and thick, filled with anger and hurt and mistrust. And it was all because of her. She suddenly felt ill. Clutching her stomach, she burst into tears, then fled out the back door.

Visit the Official Sweet Valley Web Site on the Internet at:

http://www.sweetvalley.com

THE BIG NIGHT

Written by
Kate William

Created by
FRANCINE PASCAL

BANTAM BOOKS
NEW YORK · TORONTO · LONDON · SYDNEY · AUCKLAND

RL 6, age 12 and up

THE BIG NIGHT
A Bantam Book / July 1998

Sweet Valley High® is a registered trademark of Francine Pascal.
Conceived by Francine Pascal.
Produced by Daniel Weiss Associates, Inc.
33 West 17th Street
New York, NY 10011.
Cover photography by Michael Segal.

ISBN: 0-553-49232-2

Published simultaneously in the United States and Canada

Bantam Books are published by Bantam Books, a division of Bantam
Doubleday Dell Publishing Group, Inc. Its trademark, consisting of the
words "Bantam Books" and the portrayal of a rooster, is Registered in U.S.
Patent and Trademark Office and in other countries. Marca Registrada.
Bantam Books, 1540 Broadway, New York, New York 10036.

PRINTED IN THE UNITED STATES OF AMERICA

OPM   0 9 8 7 6 5 4 3 2 1

To Keely Alexandra Schafer

Chapter 1

"Devon? What are you doing here?" Elizabeth Wakefield felt a shiver skitter down her spine as she stared at the cold, hard expression in Devon Whitelaw's slate blue eyes.

"I should be asking you the same thing," Devon snapped. "I thought we were meeting for dinner."

An unseasonably cool wind whipped the skirt of Elizabeth's white dress around her legs, and granules of sand pelted her ankles. She'd come to the beach to meet her ex-boyfriend, Todd Wilkins, and tell him it was over between them. Todd had sent her flowers and asked her to meet him here, but he hadn't bothered to show. Meanwhile Elizabeth had waited around like a fool, making herself late for the date she *wanted* to keep—her date with Devon. Elizabeth was cold and hungry, and she was already angry at Todd. She wasn't in the mood for Devon's accusatory remarks.

1

She squared her shoulders and stared back at him. "Listen, Devon, Todd invited me—"

"Todd didn't send you that invitation, I did!" Devon bellowed. "I wanted to see who you'd choose—me or your old boyfriend. And here you are, so I guess I found out!"

"You did what?" Elizabeth staggered backward as if she'd been punched. Devon had deceived her?

A cloud passed above, blocking out the moon, and Elizabeth shivered, suddenly feeling cold as the blackness enveloped her.

"*I* sent you the invitation," Devon said, his voice echoing harshly across the empty beach. "I was all ready to ask you to go to the prom, but then I saw how you acted when you saw Todd with that girl Courtney." Devon ran his hand through his hair. "I had to know if you really wanted him, if you only agreed to have dinner with me because Todd was already taken." His voice dropped an octave, becoming more pained. "And it looks like I was right. I was just a consolation prize. Instead of meeting me, you ran back here to Todd. So it was him you wanted all along."

Elizabeth felt a shocked sob rise up in her throat. She *had* been upset when Todd brought his ex-fling, Courtney Kane, to a Sweet Valley High prom committee meeting. But it hadn't been for the reasons Devon assumed. And now he was sending her fake invitations to find out the truth?

Why couldn't he have just asked her what she was feeling?

Elizabeth sucked in a shaky breath, blinking back tears. "I can't believe you tricked me like that, Devon. I did come here to see Todd, but I came to tell him we were through—that I was done with his game playing!" She glared at Devon's angular face, stunned she'd been so wrong about him. Her sweet, loving Devon had turned out to be a major waste! "But it looks like games are right up *your* alley. So now I'm through with you too!"

Furious, she spun around and stalked toward her car. Just when she thought she'd found some-one really special, someone she wanted to start a whole new life with, he turned out to be a snake.

Devon grabbed her arm. "Wait a minute, Liz. There's no way I'm letting you go until you hear me out." He paused, and Elizabeth tensed, ready to bolt the minute he released her. Then he lowered his voice and loosened his hold, gently massaging the place where he'd grabbed her. "Elizabeth, I only did what I did because . . . because I love you so much."

His voice broke on the last words, and Elizabeth closed her eyes for a second, feeling her heartbeat accelerate. Then she looked up, studying him and wondering if he was still playing with her. But his blue-gray eyes were filled with sincerity, the stony cold replaced by a sparkle that reminded her of the ocean at sunset. He spoke softly, his

3

words filled with tenderness and regret. "I really am sorry, Liz. When I saw how you reacted when Todd showed up with Courtney, I freaked. I thought you didn't want me." He dropped his head and stared at the ground, and Elizabeth's heart clenched. "All my life it's been like that. No one really cared," Devon said quietly. "I just didn't want to be your consolation date."

Elizabeth swallowed, remembering the things he'd told her about his family. He'd been a loner most of his life, staying with housekeepers and nannies while his parents traveled. Then his mother and father had died in an accident and he'd crossed the country, living with different relatives along the way. But none of them had really wanted him until he'd come to Sweet Valley and found Nan Johnstone, the one person who truly cared for him.

"That's not what you would have been, Devon." She felt her shoulders slump. The constant war of emotions going on within her was draining. "I admit I was shocked when I saw Todd with Courtney. But that's because it was *Courtney*. You don't know her the way I do, Devon. She's pulled some nasty stunts in the past. She's dangerous."

Devon glanced at his shoes, then back at her, remorse filling his eyes. "I didn't know."

"But then I thought about the whole thing, about us, and I knew it was right. And I was glad Todd was moving on." She shrugged. "I thought

4

the prom would be a way to start a new phase of my life . . . with you." She fidgeted with her hands, her breath catching.

Devon's expression changed from apprehension to hopefulness to vulnerability in a matter of seconds. She thought she saw a tear in his eye, and her heart squeezed.

"I was planning to tell Todd it was over between us. I came here to give him back this ring— to say good-bye to Todd forever." Elizabeth shook her head sadly, wiping her eyes with the back of her hand as tears seeped out and rolled down her cheeks. "I really *wanted* to go to the prom with you, Devon."

Devon looked stunned, guilty, and ecstatic all at once. Suddenly he dropped to one knee and took Elizabeth's hand in his. "Liz, I'm sorry, really I am." Elizabeth's anger evaporated at the husky tone of his voice. "I know I was being stupid earlier. Please forgive me and say you'll go to the dance with me."

The moon reemerged from the clouds, and Devon's face was bathed in its soft light. She could see the hope and sincerity glistening in his eyes. Maybe she should give him another chance.

"Please, Liz," he said softly. "I promise, if you go with me, I'll never let you down again."

He brushed his fingertips across her knuckles, and Elizabeth's heart melted into a puddle of longing. Smiling, she wrapped her fingers around

Devon's, a tingle of excitement racing up her spine. *Devon, a new beginning, the junior prom—maybe dreams do come true.*

"OK, Devon," Elizabeth said, pulling his hand to her mouth and planting a soft kiss on his fingers. "I'd love to go to the prom with you." She narrowed her eyes and gave him a warning look. "But no more games."

Devon stood, then pulled her into his arms. Elizabeth felt his heart pounding as he pressed her against his chest in a tight embrace. "I promise, no more games, Liz. Not ever."

Then he lowered his face and Elizabeth closed her eyes, absorbing the husky scent of his cologne. Just before their lips melded in a fiery kiss, he whispered, "I love you."

Her heart purred in contentment. Her junior prom was going to be perfect.

"Can you believe it, Li? We've been dreaming about prom night for years, and it's finally here!" Jessica Wakefield stretched her slender body into one of the lounge chairs beside the Wakefield pool and massaged a generous portion of sunscreen over her flawless skin.

Her best friend, Lila Fowler, dropped down into a chair beside her and dumped a stack of the latest fashion magazines at her feet. "Yeah. I remember when we were in second grade, we used to play Prom Queen at recess. And now here we are—the two most exquisite girls at Sweet Valley High, getting ready to make an appearance on the big night." Lila fluffed her silky brown hair around her shoulders, arching her bikini-clad body into a perfect model's pose. "I feel like we should have reporters writing a feature story on us—you know, something like, 'Follow Lila Fowler and Jessica Wakefield, two of Sweet Valley's most chic teens, as they prepare for the gala of the century.'"

Jessica batted her lashes. "Maybe they'll spot us as we step out of the limo tonight just like they do at the Grammy Awards. We might end up on the news after all."

They both erupted into giggles. "Just think. That goody-goody twin of yours is in class right now," Lila said, rolling her eyes in disgust.

Jessica shook her head morosely and made a clicking sound with her tongue. "Really. It's unbelievable the school only gave us a half day off to get ready for tonight. There's just so much to do!" She waved her hands dramatically. "Don't the teachers understand fashion at all? You can't achieve the right look with just five minutes; it takes time to cultivate true style. And we're it!"

"I know." Lila turned over to lie on her stomach. "At least we were smart and took the entire day off. And if I'm going to live up to my fabulous image, I *have* to put the finishing touch on my tan. I couldn't possibly show up with strap lines on my back! Not wearing a Rafael Bartucci original."

Jessica nodded, holding out one arm in front of her and examining her skin. "Exactly. There *are* priorities in life. I intend to look like a princess, not like the ghost of Sweet Valley High's prom."

Lila's laughter filled the air as she peeled open a magazine to a section on makeup tips. "Maybe we'll find some ideas in here for tonight. I still haven't decided how to do my hair. And should I wear Sinfully Red lipstick or that Daring Plum?"

"Why don't we do our hair together?" Jessica suggested.

Lila examined her nails. "Are you kidding? I've got an appointment for the works at three." She pointed to a picture of a beautiful redhead wearing her hair in a sophisticated chignon and twisted her mouth in concentration. "That's classy looking. You know, I still don't understand how your sister will ever be ready on time. Even with my hairdresser, I'm going to be cutting it close."

"You know Liz," Jessica said, rolling her eyes heavenward, "she'll run in and throw herself together. She probably won't even curl her hair. Simple and style free, that's my sister." Jessica dropped her face forward, letting her hair fall over one eye. "Of course, maybe that's for the best. There wouldn't be room for both of us to be stunning and elegant."

Jessica and Lila giggled again, then Lila drew stars beside the eyeliners, lipsticks, and eye shadows she preferred. Jessica's thoughts strayed to her twin sister. Elizabeth was such a bore sometimes, she was probably actually concentrating on her classes right now instead of daydreaming about the prom.

Although the twins looked exactly alike, with their slender athletic builds, shoulder-length blond hair, and blue-green eyes, inside they were polar opposites. They had different tastes in just about everything—especially clothes and guys. Jessica liked to wear flashy, colorful styles and all the latest trends, but Elizabeth always chose conservative, classic styles like polo shirts and khakis.

Elizabeth was a serious student who wouldn't miss a day at school, not even for the prom. She even enjoyed homework, which Jessica considered a major nuisance to her busy social life. School was simply an avenue to meet boys, plan social events, and gather friends. While Elizabeth worked on the school newspaper, Jessica would rather be *featured* in the paper, preferably in a front-page story.

Reliable Elizabeth. She'd been dating the same guy forever—boring-as-butter Todd Wilkins. Jessica saw the world as a palette to be painted with different experiences. And different, exciting, fun-loving guys were the colors. But lately Elizabeth had wised up and shown a different side—a wild side that shocked Jessica at times. She'd dumped Todd and had a fling with a brooding hunk, Devon Whitelaw, the sexiest guy ever to move to Sweet Valley.

He'd driven in on a Harley-Davidson motorcycle and had been kicking up dirt and raising the girls' eyebrows ever since. He and Todd had even fought over Elizabeth, and then Elizabeth had totally freaked and broken up with both of them. But her stint as a single woman hadn't lasted long. With the major event of the year coming up, Elizabeth had been forced to think about a date. And she'd chosen the hunk on the bike.

Normally Jessica would have been cheering Elizabeth on, but unfortunately, Elizabeth had chosen to flirt with the one guy Jessica found totally irresistible. And perfect for *her*.

"I can't wait to see my date in his tux," Lila said, letting out an exaggerated sigh. "Tall, dark, and handsome—just like in the movies."

"Me too," Jessica agreed, hardly able to contain her excitement as she thought about her own dream date. "The guys at Sweet Valley High will be sorry they scorned Jessica Wakefield when they see me walk in, escorted by the most charming guy in southern California. And he *doesn't* go to SVH."

Lila giggled. "Yeah, imagine the two of us not having the prize dates of the prom. Now that would go down in history."

Jessica nodded, a secret smile playing on her lips, as she remembered the ad she and Lila had placed for dates in the local school newspapers. They'd received a mountain of responses and conducted interviews at the Fowler Crest mansion.

Unfortunately both girls liked Jordan, the cream of the date crop. Rather than fight over him, Jessica and Lila had agreed that neither one of them would ask him to the prom. But *fortunately* Jessica had immediately decided he would be *her* date no matter what, and she'd devised a plan to snag him behind Lila's back.

She'd told Lila she'd asked a guy named Davis, a gorgeous guy with green eyes and blond hair. Lila's date was a hunk named Trevor from El Carro High who wanted to go to Yale. Trevor was tall, dark, and handsome, if a little snobby for Jessica's taste.

Jordan was by far the hottest guy they'd interviewed, and he was going to be an artist one day. A romantic plan formed in Jessica's mind, and she shivered with excitement. Maybe she'd let him paint her portrait in her slinky prom dress.

She sneaked a peek at Lila and grinned devilishly. Going to the prom with Jordan was going to be almost as fun as watching her best friend turn a deep shade of envious green. She'd definitely outwitted Lila this time. Tonight, when she breezed into Lila's preprom party with Jordan, all the heads would turn, and Jessica would be in the limelight. Lila would be so jealous. And Devon would finally notice how desirable Jessica Wakefield was. Maybe he'd even realize he'd chosen the wrong twin.

The portable phone rang, interrupting Jessica's whimsical fantasies. She picked it up and propped it underneath her ear, holding out her fingernails to examine them. She'd definitely have to have a full manicure this afternoon. Her pinky had a huge chip in it.

"Liz?"

Jessica stiffened at the sound of Devon's husky voice, a familiar shot of anger surging through her. She still hadn't gotten over the sting of his rejection. When he'd first come to Sweet Valley High, she'd been determined to make him hers. She'd gone into major flirt mode and read up on motorcycles to impress him. But he'd shrugged her off and gone after Elizabeth.

Jessica had even pretended to be Elizabeth one night and had fooled him for a while. But when she kissed him, he figured out the twin switch and became incensed. Jessica just didn't get it. Instead of choosing her boring sister, he should have been grateful to have the more exciting twin.

"It's Jessica," she told Devon, her voice dripping with false sweetness.

"Oh." Devon hesitated, sounding uncomfortable. "Listen, Jessica, school just ended and I was supposed to catch up with Liz, but we missed each other."

"Yes?" Jessica tapped her fingernails on the chair.

"I need you to give Liz a message. Tell her there's been a change of plans."

"What? You're not taking her to the prom?" Jessica asked.

"Of course I am," Devon replied sarcastically. "But I want Liz to meet me at Palomar House instead of Secca Lake."

That's a relief! Jessica thought. A swanky restaurant like Palomar House would be so much better than a picnic by the lake. "Good choice, Devon. Of course I'll tell her." Jessica hung up, but the phone immediately rang again. She snatched it to her ear. What else did Devon want? "Hello."

"Hi, Jessica. This is Jordan."

Jessica shivered at the throaty sound of Jordan's voice. "Hey, you." She glanced at Lila guiltily, but her friend had her eyes closed, her hand tapping to the beat of the music pounding from the radio.

"Listen, Jess," Jordan said. "There's been a change in plans."

What is it with these guys today? Jessica thought. *It's only a few hours until the prom, and everyone's changing their plans.*

"See, my car died," Jordan continued, sounding apologetic. "Would you mind picking me up at my house?"

"Sure." Jessica could just imagine Jordan's surprise when she arrived in a fancy limo. *Tonight is going to be so wonderful.*

"Great. I'll see you this evening." Jordan's voice dropped to a sexy whisper. "And Jessica, I'm looking forward to it."

A tingle raced up Jessica's spine. "Hmmm, me too," she whispered. Noticing Lila lift her head and

13

squint at her through the bright morning sunshine, Jessica coughed to disguise her tone.

"Who is it?" Lila whispered.

"Oh, no one!" Jessica shrugged Lila's question off with a grin and hung up the phone. She froze for a moment. Was she forgetting something? Wasn't she going to write something down?

Lila propped her chin on her hand and narrowed her eyes suspiciously. "What's going on, Jess? Your face is beet red. You're blushing!"

Jessica grabbed a sun hat from the table, then yanked it over her head. "No way. I must be getting sunburned. And I can't have a red nose on prom day. Everyone would call me Rudolph!"

Lila threw back her head and laughed. "You're right. That would totally ruin your night. It would be almost as bad as getting a zit!"

"And nothing's going to spoil the prom!" Jessica said, grateful she'd distracted Lila. She laid her outstretched fingers on her lap. "Now, let's get back to the *really* important stuff. What color should I paint my nails? Passion Pink or Raspberry Red?"

Chapter 2

"Liz, that dress is dynamite," Jessica said as she glanced from her makeup mirror to her sister. Elizabeth fitted her long, flowing gown over her slender body and spun around in a circle.

"You're sure it's not too tight?"

Jessica rolled her eyes at her sister. "Liz, when are you going to learn that a dress can't be too tight when you're going out with a guy?"

Elizabeth blushed. Just as Jessica had expected, Elizabeth had run in from school, had actually worked on an article for the paper, and now she was almost dressed for the prom. Meanwhile Jessica still hadn't decided which earrings to wear! A moment of panic hit her, but she brushed it aside. The *perfect* image took time. Still, she needed to hurry or she'd be late picking up Jordan—and she definitely didn't want to miss a minute of Lila's preprom party.

"Are you sure I shouldn't have gone with the blue dress or the black one?" Elizabeth asked, arching a perfect blond eyebrow at Jessica.

"No. That gown is totally gorgeous," Jessica exclaimed. "You look positively fabulous, Liz. You'll knock Devon right off his motorcycle."

Elizabeth smiled, turning sideways in front of the mirror to check the backless gown again. "I don't think we're riding to the prom on his bike, Jess."

Jessica grinned mischievously, thinking it might be kind of cool to see that dress flowing in the wind as the motorcycle roared through the streets of Sweet Valley. The dress accentuated Elizabeth's every curve, and the soft lavender color definitely highlighted the blue-green of her eyes. *Our* eyes, Jessica corrected herself. Elizabeth had definitely given up on conservative this time. Sequins sparkled as they caught the light, and the dress shimmered with sex appeal. Jessica couldn't wait until she could borrow it. Maybe if things worked out between her and Jordan tonight—

"You're right. I'm glad I chose the lavender over the others," Elizabeth said, cutting into Jessica's thoughts. "It makes a statement. Elizabeth Wakefield is her own person."

"And a knockout too." Jessica giggled as she brushed a light coating of blush across her golden cheeks. "You look almost as good as me!"

Elizabeth shot her a look of disbelief as she

began closing the straps on her dressy black sandals. "You are too much, Jess," she said, chuckling.

Jessica scrounged through her jewelry case, holding up two different earrings, trying to choose between the rhinestone or sapphire. Then she glanced at the clock, suddenly panicking again. The limo would be here soon. She silently ticked off the list of things she needed to do. Pick up Jordan's boutonniere—check. Plenty of cash—check. Her evening bag complete with essentials, lipstick, blush, powder—check. What was she forgetting? Something—

"Girls, when you get ready, come down and let us get some pictures," their father yelled from the bottom of the stairs. "Your mom says there's a blank space on the wall, and we have to fill it."

Elizabeth and Jessica laughed. "Be down in a sec, Dad," Elizabeth called. She added simple rhinestone earrings and her gold watch, then grabbed her brush and swept it through her hair, flipping her head upside down to give her hair more body.

Jessica turned back to her own preparations, still feeling as if she'd forgotten something. *Oh, well,* she thought as she opened a tube of her favorite Mocha Mauve lipstick and dabbed the color across her lips. *Must not be too important, or I wouldn't have forgotten it.* Blotting the excess lipstick with a tissue, she examined her completed face in the mirror, searching for any imperfection that needed her attention.

Her tan was perfect, smooth and bronze, not even a strap line on her shoulders. She barely needed any makeup at all. But Jessica Wakefield wouldn't dare go to the biggest event of her life without adding vibrant touches of color to highlight her already flawless skin. A little mascara, light touches of plum eye shadow, a thread of eyeliner to highlight the deep blue-green of her eyes. Perfect. *Look out, Jordan, here I come!*

She stood and slipped into her elegant white gown, then moved back and admired the way the dress hugged her curves and the slit up the side showcased her long, golden legs.

The simple rhinestones on her dress glittered like diamonds around her slender neck, and her hairstyle, the sophisticated twist she'd worked painstakingly to create, added just the right touch of elegance. The gold clasp holding it in place had been the perfect choice, and the small tendrils falling around her face made her look exotic. Jordan would love it. He'd be nibbling on her—

"Girls!" Mr. Wakefield shouted.

"Coming!" they shouted at once.

"Hey, Liz, will you hook me in the back?" Jessica asked.

"Sure." Elizabeth fastened Jessica's dress. "You look fabulous, Jess. This is just the way I dreamed, the two of us getting dressed together for the biggest night of our lives."

For a moment Jessica felt weepy, touched by

the tender sisterly expression on Eliza...
Elizabeth's eyes were bright and shiny too, as
felt the same way. As different as they were, they
always shared a special bond, and tonight was an
important night for both of them.

Mrs. Wakefield tapped on the door and poked
her head in the room. "Hey, you two, come on; let's
get these snapshots. The limo's here!"

They laughed, hurried down the stairs, and followed their parents outside. "OK, Dad," Jessica
said, posing against the side of the sleek dark limousine. Elizabeth put her arm around Jessica's
waist, and they both flashed gorgeous smiles.

"You look wonderful," Mr. Wakefield said. "And
you'll be glad we bought a lot of film. You'll want
these pictures later so you can remember tonight."

"Like we'll need pictures," Jessica said, flipping
her hair like a runway model.

"Yeah," Elizabeth said softly. "It'll be nice to
have photos, but we won't *need* them. After all, the
prom's going to be so much fun, how could we possibly forget it?"

"Yep," Jessica said dreamily. "It's going to be a
night to remember."

Dressed to kill, Elizabeth trekked across the
trail by the lake, searching for Devon. She almost
stumbled but caught herself in time and leaned
against a tall palm tree for support, being careful
not to mess up her evening gown. She stared over

...d laughed as she remem- ...excited squeals when she'd ...o. Apparently Jessica couldn't ...her date. *So where's mine?* ...t, suddenly feeling uneasy.

...d around in case she'd missed Devon. ...ught he would already be at the lake when ... arrived. Knowing how romantic he was, she'd expected a ten-course picnic on the water or another private fireworks display like the one he'd made for her at school. But so far he hadn't even showed.

Suddenly she remembered what had happened when she'd gone to meet Todd, and she was struck with déjà vu. *No,* she thought, shaking herself, *Devon cares about me. And this night is too important to both of us for him to stand me up.*

A branch snapped behind her, and she turned, her heart racing in anticipation. But it wasn't Devon who emerged from the bushes. It was Todd.

Elizabeth's heart started to pound in her ears. What was Todd doing here? And why did he have to look absolutely gorgeous? He was dressed in a black tuxedo with a white shirt and a black bow tie, and his brown curls were slightly tousled. He hadn't spotted her yet.

"Um . . . hey, Todd," Elizabeth said.

Todd turned and his coffee brown eyes widened in surprise, then suddenly lit up as he took in her

20

appearance. Jamming his hands into the pockets of his dress slacks, he kept his distance, but his gaze raked over her from the tips of her bare toes to the tight-fitting waistline to the thin strap at her neckline. Then he finally paused, and his eyes lingered on her face. "Liz, why are you standing here in the woods with your prom dress on?"

Elizabeth shivered, old memories of Todd flooding her mind. Todd, the first time she'd seen him dressed up, the first time he'd asked her on a date, the first kiss. Then she remembered Todd bringing Courtney to the prom committee meeting, knowing she would be there, and all the hurt swelled up again.

She cleared her throat before she spoke, reminding herself that Todd had a date with Courtney and she had a new guy in her life.

"Liz?"

"I was supposed to meet Devon here before the prom," she said, refusing to look into his eyes.

"Oh." Disappointment laced his voice, and he stared at his black polished shoes.

"Why are you here, Todd?" Elizabeth scanned the area, half expecting to see Courtney Kane slither from beneath a rock. "And where's your date?"

He shifted, suddenly looking uncomfortable. "I came here because it's *our* place, Liz," he said softly. He dug his hands deeper in his pockets as his shoulders slumped. "I was feeling confused; I . . . I was missing you so much."

Elizabeth folded her arms across her waist, refusing to let him make her feel guilty. "If you were missing me, then why did you ask Courtney to the dance?"

Todd's head snapped up. "Because you were with Devon," he answered quickly.

"But Todd," Elizabeth said in confused frustration. "I didn't agree to go with Devon until last weekend. You and Courtney were official way before that."

Todd narrowed his eyes. "What do you mean? You and Devon . . . I saw him kissing your hand. . . ."

Elizabeth's brow furrowed. "When did you see that?"

"After school one day. You guys were in the hall by the bathrooms, and he—"

Suddenly realization swept over Elizabeth. "Todd, I cut my hand, and he was helping me bandage it. He hadn't asked me to go to the prom then. We were barely friends."

Todd's face registered shock, then he frowned. He looked at her as if he was searching her face for the truth.

"You made the choice, Todd; you chose Courtney," Elizabeth said quietly.

Todd looked totally miserable. "I'm sorry, Liz. I thought you and Devon were already going together."

Elizabeth's heart squeezed at the sincerity in his voice and the puppy dog look in his brown eyes. She and Todd shared so many memories—dancing under the stars at the beach, splitting chocolate shakes at the Dairi Burger, cuddling together in the den and watching old movies. She felt as if she'd been with Todd her whole life.

But tonight was supposed to be a night of new beginnings, Elizabeth remembered in a rush, a night to start a scrapbook of memories with Devon and to close the book on Todd.

"Liz, I can't believe it all happened like this." Todd shook his head sadly. "I always thought we'd go to the prom together."

"I thought so too," Elizabeth admitted.

Todd stared at her, longing and regret shining in his eyes. "I guess I really messed up our chance, didn't I?"

Elizabeth smiled gently. "It's not your fault. But it is too late. I'm with Devon now."

Todd waved his hand toward the deserted woods. "Then where is he, Liz?"

Elizabeth bit her lip and checked her watch. "He should be here any minute." But doubts began to seep through as she searched the darkness. *Yeah, Devon, where are you?*

Chapter 3

Jessica leaned back against the plush interior of the limousine and sighed in contentment. She noticed pedestrians and several people in their cars staring at the classic lines of her posh transportation. This was the life Jessica Wakefield was meant for—first-class style. She inhaled the scent of the cream-colored leather upholstery and ran her fingers over the crystal ice bucket filled with sodas and sparkling cider, imagining the totally stunned expression on Jordan's face when he walked out and saw this baby. And Lila's when she saw the two of them arriving together! Her excitement bubbled over into giddy laughter. Things couldn't get any better.

The driver maneuvered onto Jordan's street and practically slid into his driveway, smooth as glass. Jessica leaned forward, checking herself in the mirror.

She looked incredible! The driver opened the door for her and she climbed out, gracing the tall, gray-haired man with one of her charming smiles as she started to saunter up the sidewalk. She made sure to sway her hips seductively, just in case Jordan was watching from his window.

But suddenly another stretch limousine pulled into the drive and parked right behind hers. A very familiar-looking limo. *Lila's limo*.

Jessica's eyes widened in shock as the driver opened the door and Lila Fowler's face appeared in the doorway of the backseat. Lila climbed out, her sleek figure encased in a long black dress that accentuated the richness of her dark brown hair and made her look positively exotic. Jessica froze, stunned as her supposed best friend took out a small compact to check her makeup. What was going on? What was Lila doing here?

Suspicions quickly mounted, and a horrible revelation dawned on her. Lila had tricked her! A feeling of doom slammed into her chest, and she started walking faster, determined to claim *her* date. At least Lila hadn't noticed her yet; she must have thought Jordan had rented the other limo. If she could only reach the door, get Jordan into the car . . .

She stumbled when the heel of her shoe caught in a crack in the pavement but managed to regain her balance and practically lunged for the porch. Just as she was about to reach it, she glanced over her shoulder and saw Lila look up. Her friend's eyes widened in disbelief, then darkened with anger. For a brief second their gazes locked like two enemies preparing for battle.

Then Lila sprang into action. Slinging her purse over her shoulder, she immediately started running up the sidewalk, her steps made small and awkward by her tight, hip-hugging dress and two-inch heels.

Jessica's temper skyrocketed. This was prom night. She couldn't stand here and let Lila ruin it. Bolting forward, she climbed the two porch steps and reached for the door, but Lila hurried up beside her, heaving and panting. They dove for the doorbell at the same time. Glaring at each other, they raised their hands and punched their fists toward the door at the exact moment it swung open. Jessica gasped. Lila sputtered. They both clutched for something to hold on to. Aiming for control, Jessica straightened and stared in utter shock at the gorgeous guy who was supposed to be her date.

Jordan was standing in the doorway, wearing a pair of wrinkled Lakers boxers and a tattered, faded gray T-shirt with a hole in the side. He was eating a hot dog—a very messy, greasy, smelly chili dog with mustard dripping off the sides.

"But wha . . ."

"Jordan . . ."

Lila and Jessica both began speaking at the

same time, neither one able to utter a coherent sentence. Jordan held up his hand to silence their feeble attempt at communication. He propped himself against the doorjamb and wiped a dollop of gooey sauce from his bottom lip.

Jessica shuddered. Lila winced. Jordan chowed down another bite, ignoring the chili and mustard as it dribbled on his already grungy shirt.

"I'm ready," Jessica announced in a wavering voice.

"Let's go," Lila added.

Jordan snorted, then wiped his hand on his boxers. Jessica grimaced as an onion dropped and landed on his thigh and he scooped it up with his finger and popped it into his mouth. "I'm not going anywhere," Jordan said. "But I thought you two should meet here because you'll make perfect dates—for each other." His perfect mouth deepened into a frown, and he stuffed the rest of the hot dog in his mouth.

"But Jordan, we have a date," Jessica whispered.

"And so do we!" Lila protested, her voice shaky.

"I can't believe how totally *moronic* you two are—both asking me to go to the prom behind each other's backs. I thought you were friends." Then, without saying another word, he slammed the door in their faces. Jessica and Lila jumped backward at the resounding thud.

Jessica's pulse careened off the charts. Her first inclination was to pound on the door, force Jordan to open it, then demand he escort her to the prom as he'd promised—the pig! She glanced at Lila's livid face and reconsidered. Besides, she wouldn't show up dead at any kind of function with a guy dressed the way Jordan had been. And he was smelly too. Yuck!

But suddenly Jessica realized she was without a date—gross or otherwise—for the biggest night of the year. "I can't believe it! Lila, you sneaky, no good—"

"Me?" Lila shrieked. "What about you? All that talk about the perfect date. We spent all day together tanning and planning for tonight, and you didn't say a word!"

"Neither did you!" Jessica accused. "Now the prom is totally ruined! And it's all your fault!"

"My fault? I'm not the only one who went back on our deal here, Wakefield."

"Whatever, Li. He was perfect for me in the first place. You should've stepped aside anyway, and now I don't have a date for the prom." Jessica's heart was pounding so hard, she thought it was going to explode. She narrowed her eyes to slits. "This is the lowest thing you've ever done, Lila Fowler. If I show up dateless, I'll be the laughingstock of Sweet Valley High. Especially when my own twin had guys fighting over her!"

Lila's lower lip trembled, and she let out a raspy breath, her pale skin turning slightly green. For a minute they simply stared at each other, the tension racing between them as hot and wired as an electrical storm.

Jessica finally expelled the pent-up air in her lungs and glanced back at the limo driver, feeling defeated and hopeless. "Guess we're all dressed up with nowhere to go," she mumbled, her voice brittle with unshed tears.

"Yeah. The dateless duo." Lila wrung her hands together. Her own voice sounded suspiciously close to tears. "But I do have someplace I have to go—my house. The guests are probably already waiting." Lila rolled her eyes. "Your sister and her friends are so punctual, they're probably already unfashionably early."

"Oh, no. Liz!" Jessica slapped her hand over her forehead and groaned.

"What now?" Lila asked snidely as she picked her way along the cobblestoned walk.

Jessica stumbled down the steps, her anger at Lila momentarily forgotten. "I completely forgot about the message from Devon. Liz is going to kill me!"

"Well, tell her to take a number," Lila quipped.

Jessica shrugged off Lila's threats. "I'm serious, Lila. Liz will go ballistic. And so will Devon! I can't believe the message slipped my mind."

"What are you babbling about anyway? What message?" Lila asked.

"Devon called earlier and said he had a change of plans. And I forgot to tell Liz." She stopped at the limo, the expensive vehicle no longer quite as enthralling as it had been earlier.

Her stomach plummeted as she retraced the day's events. With all the excitement, with Jordan's phone call and her scheming to keep her date with Jordan a secret from Lila, she'd completely forgotten about Devon. And now Elizabeth was on her way to Secca Lake and Devon was probably sitting at one of the classiest restaurants in town, all alone. When she was getting dressed, she'd had this feeling she was forgetting something. But she hadn't been able to put her finger on it. *Why am I such a ditz?*

She wiped at the moisture dotting her forehead as she pictured Elizabeth standing at the deserted lake, dressed like dynamite in her beautiful gown, fighting the sand and bugs and waiting for Devon—who wasn't going to show—because he was miles away, expecting her to appear any minute at Palomar House. Not only was her own night ruined, but she'd ruined her sister's preprom date too.

The sound of Lila's limo purring to life behind her brought her out of her stupor. She crawled into the empty, suddenly very lonely limousine by herself, ignoring the driver's curious stare, and dropped her face into her hands with a loud, very pathetic moan.

What was she going to do now?

Elizabeth was getting nervous. She checked her watch for the hundredth time and paced back and forth, straining for the sound of Devon's motorcycle, a car, anything to signify her date had arrived. There was no sign of anyone; the woods and the beach were empty. Where was he? Surely he wouldn't stand her up.

She chanced a glance at Todd and inwardly groaned. Her ex-boyfriend's presence was confusing her even more. He had never looked more handsome than he did tonight, wearing that dark tux. And the sad, troubled expression on his face made him even more endearing.

His broad shoulders filled his tux jacket out to perfection, making him look sinfully sexy. A twinge of sadness yanked at her heartstrings.

Feeling uncomfortable with her thoughts, Elizabeth turned away and put some distance between her and Todd, reminding herself of their noncouple status. They had broken up. She was going to the prom with Devon; he was going with Courtney Kane.

"Relax, Liz. You know I don't mind waiting here with you," Todd said, sounding a bit strained himself.

Elizabeth's skin tingled at the tender way

Todd looked at her. He was always so protective and such a gentleman. "I know. I really appreciate it, Todd. But don't you need to pick Courtney up?"

Todd shrugged and leaned against a tree. "Not for another half hour." He nodded toward the bushes, and Elizabeth noticed the darkening sky. The sun had almost completely faded, another reminder of how late Devon was. "Besides, I'm not leaving you here alone at night."

"I'll be fine, Todd. I know Devon will be here any second."

"You're probably right." Todd frowned. "But call me a sexist. A deserted beach is *not* the safest place for a girl to be alone, even for a few minutes." He leaned toward her, twisting his face into a mischievous expression. "The boogeyman might come and get you."

Elizabeth laughed, instantly relaxing as the old familiar Todd surfaced. He always had a way of making her smile, of easing the tension when she took things too seriously. Which was way too often, as Jessica constantly reminded her.

Then she noticed Todd glancing around as if he was getting nervous too. Was he worried about Courtney? Or Devon? What if he showed up and they got in another fight?

"Come on," Todd said, motioning for her to follow him. "We might as well sit down and enjoy the stars while we wait on your date."

Elizabeth let out a sigh and gave a slight nod. She followed as Todd led the way to a clearing in a rocky area where they had a magnificent view of the sunset. All the while she kept her eyes peeled for Devon.

Todd knelt, brushed the sand from a stone, shrugged out of his jacket, and laid it over the rock. "A clean seat for madam." He bowed dramatically, and Elizabeth chuckled.

"Thank you, kind sir." She curtsied, then giggled nervously. What if Devon did show up now? What would he think?

"Look," Todd said, pointing to the bank where someone had left a sand castle. "Remember that time we were on the beach at night and you stepped in a big hole someone had dug in the sand?"

Elizabeth grinned. "How could I forget? I screamed so loud, I'm surprised I didn't give the fish little heart attacks."

Todd gently tucked a strand of hair behind her ear, and Elizabeth blushed.

"Your ankle was twisted, and you tried to be so brave. But I could see you wiping the tears away," Todd said, growing serious. "I felt like a klutz," Elizabeth said, shuddering as she recalled how foolish she'd felt.

"Do you remember me carrying you all the way back to the car?" Todd asked.

"Yeah." Elizabeth laughed. "You rode me piggyback. We were only thirteen."

Todd picked up a pebble and skipped it across the water. "Hard to believe, isn't it? We've known each other that long."

Elizabeth watched the water ripple in tiny waves as the smooth stone skimmed the surface. "Yeah, since we were tiny."

A long, tense silence stretched between them, and Elizabeth sighed, hating that things had become so awkward. Todd looked at her, then away, and she knew he felt as uncomfortable as she did. Then finally Todd picked up another pebble and tossed it into the water. "Remember that night we came up here and took a midnight swim?" he asked. The stone made a soft splashing sound, and Elizabeth's mind drifted back to that evening. It had been balmy and warm with lots of stars out, shimmering and glittering like diamonds in the sky—exactly like tonight.

"I can't believe you talked me into that," Elizabeth said. "The water was freezing. It took me three days to completely thaw out."

"Yeah, but we had fun keeping each other warm."

Elizabeth shivered at the memory. She automatically inched toward Todd for warmth when goose bumps skated up her arms.

"And remember, we made that cool sand castle," Todd said, growing animated. "We had moats and bridges and a barn for all the horses you wanted."

Elizabeth sighed. "I remember. You said it was a castle for a princess."

Todd reached over tentatively and traced a finger over her knuckles. "My princess."

Elizabeth's skin tingled at the tenderness in his touch. It had been so long since he'd held her, since he'd touched her. She felt like swooning, but she decided to take a deep breath of fresh air to steady herself. Instead she inhaled the musky scent of Todd's cologne. He was so close. So sweet. So warm. So comfortable.

She gazed into his eyes and saw longing, saw all the passion and love they'd once shared, remembered the sweet tenderness of their first kiss, the times he'd held her and comforted her. And her heart tightened in her chest as she felt herself fill with affection for him. Todd had been the first guy to ever make her pulse race, the first guy she'd ever truly loved.

Devon's face suddenly flashed into her mind. She closed her eyes, trying to forget those feelings she had for Todd. She was supposed to be with Devon tonight. This night was about new beginnings, not about old memories. She was just being sentimental, getting caught up in Todd's heated gaze. Devon was her new love.

She opened her eyes and checked her watch again, but her heart nose-dived when she saw the time. Devon was an hour late. Her throat suddenly clogged with tears. Letting go of Todd and the love they'd had was so hard. But she'd been ready to do that . . . for Devon.

Only Devon was a no-show. Where was he? He'd been so sincere when he'd said he wanted to go to the prom with her, hadn't he?

"Liz, you've gotten awfully quiet," Todd said in a low voice.

Elizabeth shrugged halfheartedly, her chin quivering. Todd tilted up her face and searched her eyes. "Come on, Liz. What's wrong? I can always tell when something's bothering you."

Elizabeth was torn by the tenderness in his voice. She wanted Devon. But she missed Todd too. And she'd given Todd up for Devon, but Devon wasn't here. Everything was all wrong. She dragged her gaze away from Todd, then ran a shaky finger over the shimmering beads of her dress, thinking about how much she'd looked forward to this evening, how disappointed she was Devon hadn't showed, how Todd would be going to the prom with Courtney. And suddenly everything, all the confusion she'd felt over the last few weeks crashed around her, and she burst into tears.

"Don't cry, Liz," Todd pleaded. "Are you OK?"

"No, I'm not OK," Elizabeth said, sniffling and trying to hide her face. "I've been stood up on prom night. And you . . . and I . . . everything's been so mixed up lately." She sniffled again, burying her face in her hands.

Todd drew her into his arms and hugged her close. Elizabeth leaned into his familiar warmth and let the tears fall. "I'm . . . sorry . . . ," Elizabeth sputtered between sobs. "It's just I thought this night was going to be so different. First you, then Devon—"

"Yeah, I know what you mean," Todd responded, rubbing her back in soothing strokes. "I guess nothing worked out like we thought it would."

Elizabeth nodded against his chest, soaking up the wonderful feeling of being back in Todd's arms. He had always been so dependable, so loving, someone she could count on.

"Listen, Liz," Todd said, pulling away to look into her face. "If you'll still have me, I'd love to take you to the prom."

Elizabeth saw the hesitation in Todd's eyes, but she heard the yearning in his voice, and she knew he really wanted to be with her. Then she thought about Devon, wondering what had happened. There had to be a reason he hadn't showed. He'd said they'd meet up after school and finalize their plans. But they'd missed each other—probably because Elizabeth had been impatient to get home so that she could finish her article before the prom. Maybe he thought she'd ditched him this afternoon, and he was getting back at her. It didn't seem like the kind of thing Devon would do, but then, she hadn't known him for all that long, and he had duped her once already—

"Liz?"

Elizabeth looked at Todd and felt her heart overflow with emotion. After all that had happened, Todd was still here for her. Why not go with Todd? After all, she had been torn between Todd and Devon in the first place. And Todd was here, wanting her, obviously still in love with her.

But what about Courtney?

She brushed away the last remnants of her tears. "Todd, you're forgetting something. You can't take me. You already have a date."

Todd grimaced but shrugged. "Oh, well. I can call Courtney from my car phone when we leave. I'm sure she'll understand."

"I don't know, Todd." Elizabeth recalled her first encounter with Courtney. She had wanted Todd desperately, and when Todd had gone back to Elizabeth, Courtney had been vile. "What if she doesn't understand? She might get pretty mad."

Todd shook his head. "I doubt it. After all, it's not even *her* prom."

Elizabeth hedged, still feeling anxious. "Are you sure, Todd? You did invite her. And I can just go by myself or go home."

Todd's jaw tightened. "I asked her at the last minute, and only because I thought you were going with Devon."

Devon's name brought a fresh stab of pain and

embarrassment. Elizabeth toyed with a button on Todd's white shirt and shivered in pleasure as his warm breath brushed her cheek. She didn't approve of his plan to ditch Courtney, but she *really* wanted to go to the prom with him. "Well . . . I guess it's your decision, Todd. You can deal with it however you want."

Todd wrapped a strand of her hair around his finger and kissed her softly on the cheek. Elizabeth instinctively pressed against him. "I want to take you to the prom, Elizabeth. I always have."

Elizabeth's heart raced. She remembered Todd saying he'd come here because it was *their* spot, because he'd been missing her. And she had always dreamed of going to the prom with Todd—at least until Devon had ridden into town on his Harley-Davidson with his dark looks and lonely eyes.

Todd brushed a tender kiss over her forehead and drew both her hands into his. "Liz, please say you'll go with me. You'll make me a very happy guy."

Elizabeth slid her hand up to stroke his jaw. His face felt smooth and clean shaven, and his after-shave was driving her crazy. He looked so handsome all dressed up, absolutely irresistible. She kissed his cheek with all the tenderness she'd ever felt for him, and an ache grew inside her. She wanted more; she wanted Todd to hold her and kiss her all night. "I'd love to go with you, Todd."

Then she pushed a strand of hair away from his

forehead, letting her fingers linger on his face. Todd leaned his jaw into her hand, rubbing his face against her palm. Elizabeth's heart melted. Todd's eyes darkened and stared into hers with obvious longing. She sighed and angled her face toward his, wanting his kiss.

"Let's not go to Lila's party," she whispered. "Let's just stay here until it's time for the dance."

Todd grinned, reminding Elizabeth of how totally sexy he was when he turned on the charm. "Fine with me." He pulled her into his strong arms, and Elizabeth felt his heart pounding in his chest. "As a matter of fact, I don't mind at all. It's been way too long since I've had you to myself."

Elizabeth shivered at the husky anticipation in his voice. She felt his yearning mix with her own as Todd's warm lips touched hers. A tiny hint of guilt nagged at her as she closed her eyes to accept Todd's kiss. There must be a logical explanation for Devon's neglect.

But right now I don't care, she thought as Todd's warm lips melded firmly against hers. *Right now Todd's arms feel right.*

Jessica's Passion Pink fingernails dug into the leather seats of the limo as it pulled up in front of Palomar House. After leaving the catastrophe at Jordan's, she'd decided it would be easier to find Devon and tell him about her mistake than to find Elizabeth at Secca Lake. Elizabeth could be

41

anywhere in the park, but Devon would definitely be here. And after the disaster with Lila, the last thing she wanted to do was trek around a lake in her lavish white prom dress, get sand in between her toes, and show up at Lila's party not only dateless but streaked with dirt as well.

The driver opened the door and helped her out, one gray eyebrow arched. Jessica ignored him. "I'll be back in a few minutes," she said, tossing him a confident smile she could barely manage. She was overwhelmed by the ambiance of the impressive restaurant. The white-columned structure with its private garden and waterfall oozed class. Jessica squared her shoulders and entered the ten-foot arched doorway. Wow! Devon had style. *Too bad Liz missed this!*

But at least her sister would have Devon at the dance, she thought, remembering she, Jessica Wakefield, one of the most popular girls at SVH, was going to show up stag. Her heels sank into the plush rose carpeting, and she noticed the crystal teardrop chandelier twinkling in the dim candlelight. French impressionistic paintings adorned the pale sea green walls, and the ceiling was painted a creamy mauve bordered by ornately carved white molding.

Jessica finally spotted Devon sitting at a corner table, looking lost and lonely and incredibly sexy. A gasp caught in her throat. He was unbelievable.

She'd thought Devon looked fine in a leather

jacket, but a tux made him look drop-dead gorgeous. *It isn't fair. Liz gets this, and I don't even have a date!*

Devon started to look up, and Jessica jumped behind a tall potted plant, grabbing the marble pedestal it was sitting on to steady the plant as it tottered sideways. A passing waiter carrying a tray of pasta shot her a curious look, and Jessica winked, then raised her finger to her lips to motion for him to be quiet. She pointed to Devon, and the man lifted a brow, then grinned as if he realized she wanted to surprise Devon. She peeked around the silky pointed leaves of the plant and saw Devon scanning the room for Elizabeth.

Jessica turned and stared at her reflection in a gilt-framed mirror on the wall. "OK, Jess," she said to herself. "How are you going to handle this?" She almost laughed at the pitiful look in her own eyes. It was more an expression her sappy sister would wear.

Jessica's heart skipped a beat. "Wait a minute . . ."

She pressed her hand to her cheek. If she could pass herself off as Elizabeth, she could still go to Lila's party with Devon and she wouldn't be dateless!

Sure, everyone would think "Jessica" wasn't there, but at least she'd get to experience the party without feeling like a loser. Then when she got to the prom, she'd give Devon back to Elizabeth, and Jessica could party with her

43

friends the rest of the night. Violin music began playing in the background, and she noticed Devon pivot to watch the trio of musicians. Even though she preferred jazzy rock tunes, the classical melody was utterly romantic. And Devon was *soooo* handsome.

She started forward, then froze in a moment of panic. What if Elizabeth showed up at the party? Jumping back behind the plant to rethink her plan, Jessica wrinkled her brow, considering the possibility. She saw Devon take a sip of water, then stand, looking around the room for her sister.

Nah. Elizabeth didn't really care about Lila's party. She would wait at the lake for Devon until the last minute, and they would both miss the preprom affair. Then Elizabeth, being such a predictably responsible person, would go straight to the country club.

Jessica grinned, smacking her lips in satisfaction. Poor Devon. He was probably starved. She and Devon could attend Lila's together, then she would take Devon to the prom and give him back to Elizabeth.

Elizabeth would definitely be happy when he got to the prom. *That is, if I can give him back,* Jessica thought, checking him out again.

She moved out from behind the plant, straightening her dress. She couldn't wait to spend some quality time with the hottest guy in the universe. Then she caught her reflection in the mirrored wall on the opposite side of the restaurant. She looked great, only her hair was way too sophisticated for Elizabeth. She headed for the bathroom to tone down her appearance. Devon had caught her in the act once before.

But it's not going to happen this time! Jessica decided. *This time he'll never know the difference.*

Chapter 4

Devon checked his watch for the millionth time. Where in the world was Elizabeth? He dropped the fork he'd been thumping on the table for the last twenty minutes and craned his neck to see across the room. Elizabeth's friend Maria Slater and her date were sitting at a corner table, talking and laughing and sipping coffee. Maybe Maria had talked to Elizabeth. There had to be a reasonable explanation for her lateness. He knew how much the prom meant to her and all the other kids at SVH. Maybe Elizabeth had some last minute catastrophe with the decorations to take care of. Elizabeth was so reliable. If there was a problem, she'd be the first person they'd call.

Or she could still be getting dressed. Girls took forever! Even Elizabeth, who kept her makeup and clothes simple, would be going all out tonight.

And Elizabeth was dressing up for *him*. She'd probably wear the special rose-scented perfume he'd made for her, maybe a striking dress that would bring out the vivid color of her blue-green eyes, soft slinky material that would cling to her slender, athletic figure. He couldn't wait to see her, to hold her, to kiss her—to be with her all night. She was finally his.

"At least she will be if she ever shows up," Devon muttered.

"Excuse me, sir, but are you ready to order?" The waiter gave him a sympathetic look. The swanky restaurant was packed, and Devon supposed the waiter wanted him to either eat or leave and offer up his table. Or maybe he thought Devon couldn't afford the expensive entrées. Little did he know Devon could buy the entire place if he wanted. But if Devon was going to buy a business, it definitely wouldn't be a fancy place like this. He never really patronized places like this at all, but he'd come here to make things special for Elizabeth. He'd planned to wine and dine her just like in the old movies, romance her so she wouldn't ever look at that guy Todd Wilkins again.

"Sir?" The waiter cleared this throat loudly, snapping Devon out of his thoughts.

"No, not yet," Devon said curtly, laying his napkin on the table. "Give me a few more minutes. I'm sure she'll be here." *Liz wouldn't let me down—not tonight.*

He stood and strode over to Maria's table, hoping she'd have some answers. "Uh, hi, Maria."

"Hey, Devon. Great to see you," Maria said, grinning widely. The guy sitting next to Maria glanced from Maria to him and back and curved his arm around Maria's shoulders. Maria looked great in her black formal dress, and she was always friendly. Devon could easily understand why she and Elizabeth were friends.

"Devon, this is my date, Tyler Becksmith. Tyler, Devon." She folded her slender hands on the table. "Devon's going to the prom with my friend Elizabeth."

"Hi, nice to meet you, Tyler." Devon studied Tyler's face. Something seemed familiar, but he couldn't place the guy. "You don't go to SVH, do you?" Devon asked.

"No. I actually live in New York. I know Maria from there," Tyler answered.

"Oh? So you came all the way out here to take Maria to the prom?" Devon asked.

Maria laughed. "I wish! It would be cool to inspire guys to cross the country for me."

"Hey! I would've if you had called me," Tyler said, nudging her. Then he glanced back at Devon. "I bumped into Maria at the mall last week. I was doing a shoot."

Devon narrowed his eyes, confused. "A shoot?"

"He's a model," Maria clarified.

"Oh! That's where I've seen you before!" Devon

exclaimed. "You do those cologne commercials, right?"

Tyler made a disgusted face. "Yeah. But they're so stupid, I try to forget about them."

"Not me," Maria teased. "I *can't* forget how you look playing in the surf in a pair of tight jeans."

Devon and Tyler both rolled their eyes and grinned.

"Well, anyway, Maria, I was wondering if you'd talked to Elizabeth." Devon glanced at his watch again, shaking his arm to make sure the battery hadn't stopped. "She was supposed to meet me here about an hour ago."

Maria frowned. "No. I haven't talked to her since this morning. But that doesn't sound like Liz."

"I know; that's just what I was thinking."

"Why don't you call her at home?" Maria suggested.

Devon nodded. "I was just going to do that."

Devon said good-bye, then headed to the lobby to find a pay phone. But as he rounded the corner and passed a tall silk plant a brilliant flash of white caught his eye, and he glanced toward the door. It was Elizabeth. The sight of her nearly took his breath away.

She was standing in the doorway, looking absolutely divine in a floor-length white dress with her hair falling over her shoulders. He should have known Elizabeth would wear white; it was the perfect color for her, all innocence and purity.

When she spotted him, she gave him a radiant smile that sent his blood racing through his veins, and he pulled at the tie binding his neck. It suddenly felt hot and choking. She glided over to him and kissed him on the cheek. He grinned stupidly, his pulse accelerating. Finally their special night could begin.

"I'm sorry for being late, Devon," Elizabeth said softly. "But my ditz of a sister forgot to give me your message."

Devon breathed a sigh of relief, so transfixed by her beauty, he could hardly speak. She was the most gorgeous girl he'd ever seen, and she was *his*. "It's OK, Liz," he said, gazing into her vibrant eyes. "Don't worry about it. We've got all night." He took her hand and started to guide her back to their table.

Elizabeth hesitated. "Listen, Devon, it's getting so late. We might as well head on over to the party at Lila's."

Devon paused. "Are you sure you don't want to eat first?"

"Yeah. Let's just go to the party. There'll be tons of food there."

Devon noticed Maria and Tyler leaving their table. Elizabeth was right. He didn't really care about going to Lila's, but if Elizabeth wanted to go to the party and see her friends, then he was all for it. He should have known he wouldn't have to impress Elizabeth with a fancy dinner.

He smiled to himself, his heart swelling. The two of them belonged together. And maybe after tonight Elizabeth wouldn't have any doubts either. He put his hand at the small of Elizabeth's back, feeling dizzy when his fingers connected with warm, bare skin. Even her back was perfect.

He didn't care where they spent the evening, as long as he was with Elizabeth.

Lila smiled at Ken Matthews and Olivia Davidson, deftly avoiding any conversation about her nameless date, then glided past A.J. Morgan and Suzanne Hanlon. Suzanne flitted by, giggling and talking about how cute A.J. had looked trying to put on his cuff links. Lila averted her gaze, pretending to check the buffet table to see if anything needed refilling.

"His father handed him the cuff links, and A.J. didn't even know what they were for," Suzanne said with a giggle.

Lila's preprom extravaganza was a definite success. The cook had outdone herself preparing the finest delicacies, including Lila's favorite escargot dip and clam sauce along with imported caviar. Her parents had tastefully decorated the house with crystal candleholders and silver vases filled with yellow roses. Outside, bouquets of balloons in the school colors were tied to chairs and all around the pool house. Music from her favorite CD collection poured from the speakers of the surround-sound system her parents had installed after one of her begging jags. Laughter and conversation filled the room. Excitement over the upcoming dance charged through the air like electricity, and everyone was having a wonderful time. Everyone except *her*.

"Great party," Amy Sutton said as Lila walked by. "So, Lila, where's your—"

"I'm glad you're having fun," Lila called out as she continued on her way. Amy was one of SVH's most accomplished gossips, and Lila wasn't about to let the girl get a question in edgewise.

Lila grabbed a goblet of sparkling cider from a waiter and curled her fingers around the slender flute, pasting on a phony smile. All the happy, lovey-dovey couples were making her ill. For the first time ever she wanted to leave the gaiety of the crowd and retreat to her room, where it was quiet and she could be alone to lick her wounds, but she couldn't be absent from her own party. So far she'd managed to skirt the issue of her nondate and Jessica's whereabouts, but if she left, someone would definitely notice. And that would only feed the gossip line. Caroline Pearce would be so ecstatic, she'd probably leave the prom just to blab it to the neighboring schools.

"Hi, Lila, the party's great," Maria Santelli said, strolling up with her arm hooked through Winston Egbert's. Maria looked pretty in a short royal blue dress, and she was practically gushing all over Winston. Lila wanted to gag.

53

"Yep, you pulled off a fine start for the evening," Winston said, tipping his hat. In spite of her dismal mood Lila fought a laugh at the old-fashioned tux, ruffled shirt, and top hat Winston had rented. He looked as if he'd walked straight off an old movie set. "I still think we should have had a Fred Astaire look-alike contest." Winston shrugged, deepening his voice in a fake imitation of the famous man himself. "But like all the geniuses of the world, I'm just ignored."

"Who *would* listen to you, genius or not, with that ridiculous hat on?" Maria teased, pushing the brim back from his forehead.

Lila smothered a giggle as Winston's hat slipped to one side. He caught it, then nodded at Maria. "Shall we show these people how to waltz tonight, my darling?"

Maria rolled her eyes, but Lila saw the grin she couldn't hide. Winston swept his date into his arms and swung her across the living room, skirting the crowd of classmates mingling and talking. Maria's laughter echoed through the room, reminding Lila of how alone she was.

Lila inwardly grimaced. She was actually jealous of Maria and Winston. Life had really gone downhill! She was going to kill Jessica for ruining her night. She scanned the crowd, unable to hear herself think over the noisy chatter but checked to make sure she'd spoken to everyone. She made a mental list. Ken and Olivia, Aaron Dallas and

Heather Mallone, Enid Rollins and Blubber Johnson—what a combination.

Finally, deciding she'd performed her hostess duties, she ducked outside and tiptoed into the pool house. Glancing around the comfortable, spacious room, she remembered when the fire had almost destroyed her house and she'd actually lived out here. She shivered at the frightening memories, but they faded when she remembered her short fling with Steven, Jessica's brother. She'd been frightened and alone after the fire, and Steven had comforted her. The police had actually suspected her of trying to burn down her own house, but Steven was doing an internship at the DA's office and had helped clear her name.

Too bad Steven wasn't home from college now. Maybe *he'd* have escorted her to the prom. That would have served Jessica right! Jessica hadn't liked it when Lila dated Steven. If he were in town, she'd pick up the phone and beg him to take her to the prom just to make Jessica squirm.

"Fowler."

Lila yelped in surprise, then spun around to see Jessica burst through the doorway, her cheeks flushed.

"What are you doing out here?" Jessica asked, wrinkling her brows in confusion.

"Stay away from me," Lila ordered.

"What?" Jessica froze, obviously stunned.

"I'm miserable tonight, and it's all your fault, Jessica."

Jessica rambled on as if she hadn't heard her. "Don't be ridiculous. We're going to have a great time."

"What are you talking about?" Lila asked.

"Li, you won't believe what happened. I went to Palomar House to find Devon, then I had a major brainstorm. I stole Devon for the party. I told him I was Liz, and he came here with me!"

"You did what?" Lila slapped her hand over her chest in shock. "Jess, that's low even for you!"

Jessica shook her head vigorously. "No, you don't understand. I'm going to give him back to Liz after the party, and she'll still go to the prom with him, but for now he's mine! Six-foot plus, incredible blue eyes and all."

"I can't believe you," Lila said. "First you try to sneak Jordan out from under me, then you take your own sister's boyfriend."

Jessica's face wilted as if she was offended. "It's not like that." She launched into a rushed explanation of what had happened. "When I stepped inside the restaurant, I realized Liz and Devon had already missed dinner, so why not bring Devon to the party?" Jessica giggled excitedly. "Devon looked so lonely, and I didn't want him to think Liz had purposely left him there like that."

"But Elizabeth didn't do it on purpose," Lila argued. "It was your fault, Jess."

"Oh, well, it was just a silly mistake!" Jessica answered flippantly. "I figure when Devon doesn't show at the lake, Liz will probably go straight to the dance. After your party I'll take Devon there and return him to Elizabeth. It'll be perfect."

"You are unbelievable," Lila said, rolling her eyes.

Jessica smiled as if Lila had complimented her. "When I give Devon back to Elizabeth, I'll tell her about my mess up and how I went to Palomar House in her place so Devon wouldn't think he'd been stood up. Then Liz and I can switch dresses, and everything will be fine."

"You really think your levelheaded sister will agree to that?"

"Of course," Jessica said without batting an eyelash. "She'll probably even thank me!"

Lila tapped her head with her fingers. "You are truly delusional, Jess."

"Well, she *should* thank me." Jessica's eyes twinkled mischievously. "That is, unless I decide to keep him for myself, of course."

"I don't know what you're babbling about, Jess. If you give up Devon at the prom, which you *will* have to do once you see Liz, you and I are still going to be dateless."

"Then we'll just steal other dates," Jessica supplied happily.

Lila rubbed her hand over her temple, her mind reeling. Sometimes the breadth of Jessica's scheming mind astounded her.

"It could work," Jessica said with renewed vigor.

Lila studied Jessica quietly, thinking for a moment. "Think about who you might end up with," Jessica suggested in a wicked voice. "Haven't you seen any cute guys at your party?"

Hmmm, that guy Penny Ayala snagged looked pretty hot, Lila thought.

"Come on, Li. It's prom night! Let's have fun!" Jessica's jovial mood was starting to rub off on Lila. She began to see the possibilities. "OK, Jess. I'll go along with you at the party."

Jessica pumped her fist in a victory sweep, turned, and flitted toward the house, her hips swaying in her tight white dress. Lila straightened her back, wet her lips, tossed her hair over her shoulders, and followed, adding a sexy lilt to her own walk as she headed toward Penny Ayala's date.

Maybe this night won't be so bad. . . .

Devon was determined to make tonight so incredible, Elizabeth would never forget it—or him. As he walked into the imposing Fowler Crest mansion he knew most people would be impressed with the magnificence of the estate, but Devon remembered his parents' wealth and how empty his life had been in their huge, rambling house. He followed Elizabeth and passed the ambiance of Lila's home off with barely a notice. Money and expensive things didn't mean anything. People did.

And the only thing that mattered to him tonight

58

was the special person beside him—Elizabeth Wakefield.

"Wow, Devon. Lila's house looks great tonight. Look at all the balloons."

"Yeah, it's nice," Devon said with a simple shrug.

Elizabeth was beaming as she waved to some of their classmates. "The party's packed. Everyone's here!" Elizabeth squealed with excitement. Devon immediately spotted Maria Slater and Tyler in the buffet line. Maria waved, but Elizabeth gave her a brief smile, practically ignoring her. Maria's eyebrows furrowed, and she shot Devon a questioning look.

But before Devon could figure out what had happened, Elizabeth waved to a group of the cheerleaders and pulled him through the crowded room, smiling and speaking to half a dozen guys he hadn't met, including a pack of football players who almost dwarfed him in size. A spark of jealousy ignited within him, but he remembered he was the guy Elizabeth had chosen, and his chest swelled with pride. *Eat your heart out, guys,* he thought with a smug grin. *I've got Liz for tonight. And maybe forever, if I play my cards right.*

"Hey, you guys!" Winston called out, tipping his top hat.

Devon stopped and grinned at Winston's crazy outfit. "Great tux, Winston."

"You look snazzy yourself," Winston replied. "And whoa, Liz. Awesome dress."

"Thanks, Winston," Elizabeth said, glancing at Maria Santelli, who stood laughing and talking with Blubber. Blubber waved his beefy hands in animation. He was obviously in the middle of telling a football story.

"You definitely went all out tonight," Elizabeth said.

"Hey. You only have one junior prom," Winston said with a smile.

As Maria Santelli joined in on the conversation Devon saw Enid weaving her way through the crowd toward them. She had a sad, sort of desperate look on her face, so when Elizabeth spotted Enid, Devon expected Elizabeth to head straight toward her friend. But Blubber intercepted Enid, and her face fell. Elizabeth just turned her back on her friend and continued talking with Winston.

"Maybe you should go talk to Enid, Liz," Devon whispered. "She looks like she needs some help over there."

"Enid can take care of herself," Elizabeth answered. For a moment Devon was taken aback by Elizabeth's abrupt answer, but then she smiled at him, and he knew she hadn't meant anything by it. She probably just thought Enid should get to know Tad better since they did have to spend the whole evening together.

Two giggly girls who Devon recognized from the cheerleading squad joined the little crowd and Elizabeth. She laughed and chatted with them for several minutes. Devon hadn't known Elizabeth was close with those girls. Maybe she was doing a story on school spirit for the newspaper.

"Lila sure knows how to throw a party, doesn't she?" Winston asked. "Her mom lived in Paris for a while. One time she had this fancy French dinner for everyone. It was great. Except none of the guys liked the quiche."

"Sounds cool," Devon said. *And pricey,* he thought.

"They have a beach house too," Winston added. "After homecoming our freshman year they let everyone sleep over."

"That sounds like fun," Devon said. "I wish I'd been here then." *With Elizabeth,* he added silently.

"Come on, Win, you owe me a dance," Maria said, dragging Winston away.

"Sorry, man," Winston called over his shoulder. "Duty calls." Devon laughed as Winston tripped over his own feet and had to grab his girlfriend for support.

"I'm dying of thirst," Elizabeth said, brushing her hand over his arm. "Let's go get something to drink, Devon."

"I'll get it for you," Devon offered, ready to cater to her every wish.

"You're so sweet," Elizabeth whispered. "And you look great. You remind me of James Bond in that tux."

Devon's heart did a crazy drumroll, almost

banging out of his chest. James Bond was his favorite film icon. The guy was so smooth. He gulped in an attempt to calm himself and gave Elizabeth a soft kiss on her cheek. "Be right back with your drink."

In a matter of seconds he returned, carrying a crystal goblet of punch and one of sparkling cider. He should have asked Elizabeth which one she preferred, but since he hadn't, he'd brought both. The way his hands were shaking, it was a wonder he hadn't spilled them and broken the hundred-dollar glasses on his way over.

"Thanks, Devon," Elizabeth said, deftly taking the slender glass of sparkling cider from him. He tossed the punch down his own dry throat to calm his nerves.

Lila sauntered over and planted one hand on her hip. "Hi, Devon, I hope you're having a good time."

Devon's hand clenched around the glass. Lila was pretty cool, but her eyes were shining as if she was up to something. "Oh, yeah, great party, Lila."

Lila batted incredibly dark lashes at him, and he winced, wondering how she could flirt with him right in front of Elizabeth. Elizabeth slid her arm through his, almost in a possessive gesture. A gesture he didn't mind at all. *So far, so good.*

"I'm hungry. How about you?" Elizabeth whispered.

"Sure. I forgot we missed our dinner. I'll go get us some food."

"Don't be gone too long."

He swallowed nervously and backed away with a silly grin on his face. "I'll be right back."

Out of the corner of his eye he saw Lila shake her head at Elizabeth and laugh. He made it to the buffet, then stood behind Ken Matthews and A.J. Morgan, who had loaded their plates with everything from steamed shrimp to tiny chocolate éclairs, which looked delicious. Devon was so hungry, he could eat about a dozen of them. Not knowing exactly what Elizabeth liked, he filled her plate with a sampling of everything, making a silent vow to use this night to discover as much about her as possible.

"Man, you must be as hungry as me," Blubber said, gesturing toward his own heaping plate. Devon chuckled. Blubber must weigh around two-forty, and Devon had heard the linebacker wasn't too smart, but he was a great football player.

"Enid and I ate at this fancy restaurant." Tad chuckled. "But to tell you the truth, they didn't serve portions big enough for a baby, much less me. We ate something that looked like it came straight from the bottom of the ocean—raw and slimy." Blubber made a disgusted face. "By the time I fished out a little piece of meat that wasn't even as big as my thumb, I was worn out. And still starving."

Devon laughed good-naturedly. "I know what you mean." He gestured toward Elizabeth. "You and Enid want to come over and hang out?"

"Sure. I think Enid would rather talk to Elizabeth than me." Blubber ran a hand through his brown hair and managed a little smile, then ambled over to get Enid. Devon instantly felt bad for the guy. It must be tough going to the prom on a first date. There was so much added pressure.

Devon found Elizabeth and handed her a plate. "I wasn't sure what you liked, so I brought a bit of everything," he said, eyeing Maria Slater from across the room. She gave them another strange look as if she was confused about something, but he didn't have a clue. And he didn't understand why Elizabeth kept talking to Lila and all those cheerleaders. She hadn't even mentioned Maria or Enid all night.

Enid and Blubber came up beside them. "Hey, Liz. You finally made it," Enid said, looking relieved.

"Oh, hi, Enid. Tad," Elizabeth said politely. "There was a little mix-up about where we were supposed to meet, but Devon and I are here now." She stabbed a shrimp with her toothpick, nibbled the edge, then grabbed his arm and looped her hand through it. "Come on, Devon. I need to go see Olivia about something." She practically dragged him away from Enid and Tad.

"What's wrong?" Devon asked once she'd finally stopped beside the dessert table. "Did you and your friends have a fight?"

Elizabeth stared at her shoes. "Yeah, something like that." She pasted a quick smile on her face that didn't quite reach her beautiful eyes, and he realized she was trying to hide her hurt feelings from him. Then she spoke in a hushed, intimate voice. "But I don't want to think about it tonight, Devon. I just want to have a good time."

Devon's heart went out to Elizabeth. She was obviously so upset over her argument with Maria and Enid that she wasn't even acting like herself. He vowed right then that he would do everything he could to make the night perfect for her. Elizabeth deserved the best.

Chapter 5

"Hey, you guys, we'd better get going or we'll miss the prom," Lila announced above the noisy chatter. Cups and cutlery clinked as students finished their drinks and food and the servants collected them.

"Thanks for inviting us," Penny said.

Penny's date didn't even look at Lila; he just grabbed Penny's hand and hurried out the door. So much for stealing that guy! Lila had tried her best to break into their conversation a few minutes earlier, but he seemed to be totally taken with Penny. Imagine! Lila Fowler being passed over for a mousy newspaper editor. Being brushed off by two guys in one night was almost more than she could take.

"Great party," Heather Mallone said, slipping past Lila with Aaron Dallas hanging on her arm. Heather flipped her white blond hair over her shoulder and gave Lila a snotty smile.

Lila pretended sweetness. "Nice of you to come, Heather."

She couldn't let Heather or anyone else see how miserable she really felt inside—if Jessica hadn't suggested they steal dates, she might still be out in the pool house sulking!

"This was really generous of you and your folks," Olivia said.

"Good food," Ken added. "Especially those hot things."

"The spiced sushi," Lila interjected.

Ken's face turned red, and he clutched his throat. "Oh, my God. I didn't know I was eating raw fish! Can we have plain burgers next time?"

Olivia swatted his arm, and Lila waved to them as they made a hasty exit. "Bye, you guys, see you at the prom," Lila called after them. They were disgusting, hanging all over each other like two lovesick puppy dogs. Lila watched them walk hand in hand down the drive, their bodies almost inseparable. Who'd ever have thought that Miss Artsy Fartsy, poetic leftover from the hippie days, would have fallen for one of the leading jocks?

Her other guests started to mill toward the door, the entryway filling with girls gathering their wraps and purses, guys slapping each other on the back and talking about the upcoming dance and the yacht the school had hired to take out the kids for an all-night after-the-prom cruise. It was really a dream evening—too bad she didn't have a dream date to escort her.

"You outdid yourself this time, Miss Fowler," Winston commented as he escorted Maria through the door.

"Yeah, thanks for having us," Enid said as she and Tad Johnson followed Winston out. Lila shook her head—another odd combination. Blubber was a great football player, but his grades had almost gotten him kicked off the team. He was the last person she'd have expected to see Elizabeth's studious friend Enid dating. Of course, Enid didn't exactly look like she wanted to be with Tad either.

Lila grimaced. Maybe dateless wasn't as bad as going to the prom with a guy nicknamed Blubber.

Other kids offered polite thanks as they filed out, and some of the kids loitered on the lawn, talking and cracking jokes while others lingered beside the limos they'd rented.

"Thanks for inviting us," Devon said.

Lila gave Devon one of her most charming smiles. Jessica simply grinned and leaned against Devon, then mouthed, "Isn't he a hunk?"

Amy Sutton waved, and Lila yelled good-bye to her, smiling. But Lila's smile froze when a familiar Mustang convertible screeched to a stop in front of the house. Courtney Kane jumped out in an impossibly tiny red dress covered in shiny sequins that glittered in the darkness like a sky full of stars. Her mahogany hair was swept up in a silver comb, but she looked so mad, Lila could swear her smoky eyes were actually *smoking*.

"What's she doing here?" Jessica whispered.

Lila shrugged. "I don't know, but she sure looks mad about something."

Jessica dragged Devon out of the line of fire, and Lila folded her arms across her chest, preparing herself for a confrontation.

Courtney stormed straight toward Lila, not even pausing to say excuse me when she bumped into Maria Slater and almost knocked Caroline Pearce into a rosebush. "Where is Todd?" she asked angrily.

"I don't know," Lila answered.

"I demand you tell me where he is right this minute," Courtney said more harshly, stamping her foot like a petulant child.

"Calm down, Courtney. We haven't seen Todd." Lila took a step backward and gave Jessica a "help me" look.

Courtney glared at Jessica, her features tight with fury. She looked like a volcano about to erupt. "Where is he?"

Jessica shrugged, chewing on her lip nervously. "How should I know?"

Courtney huffed. "Oh, come on, Elizabeth. I think you do know. Todd stood me up!" She quickly blazed a trail across the lawn with her hot gaze as if she could smoke him out from his hiding spot.

"He called and said he decided he didn't want to go to the prom. Ha! Like I really believe Mr. Sweet Valley High Spirit is ditching the prom." Courtney took a menacing step toward Jessica, pointing her finger in Jessica's face. "I half expected to find Todd here with you!"

Jessica blanched, and Devon stepped in front of her protectively.

"I think you should calm down," Devon said in a slightly threatening voice.

"Don't tell me what to do," Courtney hissed.

"Look, Courtney," Lila said, taking her arm gently. "Just calm down. Todd hasn't been here at all tonight, and we don't know where he is. Why don't you come to the country club with us? That way if Todd decided to go with someone else, you can see him for yourself."

Courtney stopped, once again scanning the lawn as if she thought they might be hiding Todd behind one of the azalea bushes or limos. When she didn't spot him, she jutted her chin up in the air defiantly and nodded.

"I think I will go with you. And if Todd's there . . ." She let her words trail off as she strutted toward her car, her legs wobbling on two-inch black spiked heels. The remaining guests filtered to their cars, and the sound of motors humming and kids shouting good-bye filled the crisp night air.

Lila shook her head as Courtney jumped in her car, cranked the engine, and spun down her long drive, tires screeching. The scent of burning rubber filled the air in her wake. Relieved Courtney hadn't run over somebody, Lila glanced at Jessica. But having already dismissed Courtney's tirade, Jessica was gushing over Devon.

Hmmm . . . Elizabeth and Todd both missing, Lila thought. *Could they somehow be together?*

Wasn't anyone with the person they were supposed to be with? As the parade of vehicles left the estate everyone started to honk their horns and cheer.

Lila headed toward her own sleek white limo, smiling at the driver as he opened the door and politely helped her in.

Settling into the plush interior, she poured herself a tall bubbling glass of soda and tried to get her agitated nerves under control. Pretending it was champagne, she leaned back and tried to relax, thinking about Courtney's scene-stealing performance. *Well, if not fun, at least this prom is going to be interesting.*

Jessica settled back into the limousine with Devon, her heart fluttering as he gazed into her eyes. The purr of the engine and soft music floated around them, creating a romantic atmosphere. Jessica suddenly felt dizzy with excitement, like she was riding high in the clouds instead of cruising down a busy California street.

"Thanks for making the party special tonight, Devon."

"It was fun," Devon said. "Winston cracks me up."

"He's always been the class clown," Jessica said. "Last year he brought in fake eyeballs from a left-over Halloween party and put them in our history teacher's desk. You could hear her screaming all the way from the lab to the football field."

Devon laughed heartily. Jessica watched him, wishing things could always be this easy and comfortable between them. Wishing Devon was really her date and she didn't have to return him to her twin sister in a few short minutes. The night had only just begun.

"Boy, that girl Courtney sure was mad. I thought she was going to start a catfight with Lila right there on the front lawn."

Jessica nodded, trying to think of a way to steer the conversation away from that last scene. She didn't want to talk about Todd and Courtney because it would inevitably lead to Devon asking her, as Elizabeth, how she felt about them. Where was Todd anyway?

"Courtney's known for her temper. She looks great, but don't mess with her, or she'll eat you alive."

Devon chuckled. "I'll remember that." He scooted closer to her, their legs touching. "But I don't intend to mess with her. I've got eyes only for you, Liz."

Jessica smiled. "I feel the same way." She faked the most sincere expression she could muster. "I'm sorry about earlier, Devon. I didn't mean to make us miss our dinner."

"It's no big deal," Devon said. "It wasn't your fault you were late. Like you said, it was your ditzy sister who forgot to give you the message."

Jessica bit her lip, forcing herself not to react to the fact he had thrown her own words back at her. *Play it cool. Be Elizabeth.* "I know Jessica didn't mean to forget. She had about a thousand phone calls this afternoon. Plus she had so much to do to get ready. I can understand how it slipped her mind."

Devon shrugged. "I'm sure she had a lot to do. Still, I wish she'd told you. I wanted to take you out someplace nice. . . ." Devon blushed. "You know, to show you how much you mean to me."

Jessica's throat closed at the tender expression in his eyes. This guy was a dream come true! He wasn't just sexy, but he was so sweet! No wonder Elizabeth had dumped boring, reliable Todd for him. "Well, it was really romantic of you to make reservations, Devon. Thanks for not being angry at me. Maybe we can go to Palomar House another night."

Devon grinned. "I'd like that, Liz."

Jessica picked up his hand, playing with his fingers. When she crossed her legs, the slit in her dress parted to reveal her smooth, tanned thigh. She saw Devon swallow, and excitement skittered inside her. *Be calm and sweet like Liz,* she reminded herself. *You can't give yourself away yet.*

"I'm happy as long as I'm with you," Devon said.

"You're so understanding," Jessica said softly. Devon tipped back his head and Jessica was mesmerized by his strong, chiseled face. A stray lock of his dark brown hair fell down over his forehead, and she tentatively reached out and brushed it back.

"I'm just glad we finally have some time alone." Devon's warm gaze locked with Jessica's, and she could feel the heat racing between them. He traced a finger down the flesh at the base of her neck, and she suddenly felt giddy.

"I've been looking forward to it for days, Liz."

Jessica curled up against Devon's strong, lean body and inhaled the woodsy scent of his cologne. She wished the night could last forever. And she wished he'd say her name, Jessica, just as he'd said *Liz.* "I've been dreaming about being with you too, Devon," she whispered. She ran her hands over the lapels of his white tux jacket. "And you made it worth it. You look devastatingly handsome tonight."

Devon smiled, his slate blue eyes sparkling with humor. "You have a way with words, Ms. Wakefield. The next thing I know, you'll be spouting poetry. Maybe you'll even write a special poem about our first dance together and read it to me by the beach one night."

"Maybe," Jessica said, wincing at the reminder of her twin. Would Elizabeth really do something so geeky as to recite poetry on a date? She couldn't think of anything more sappy or moronic. She'd show Devon how tantalizing *she* could be, and she certainly didn't need Elizabeth's poetry tricks to do it.

"This prom night is going to be special, a new start for us." Devon cupped her chin with his hands and brushed his lips across her cheek.

Jessica melted against him, his words caressing her, as soft and gentle and soothing as the scent of her favorite bath oil washing over her. He combed his fingers through her hair, and she heard him sigh with contentment.

Closing her eyes, she savored being in Devon's arms as he pulled her close. *Yes,* Jessica decided, *it is going to be a new beginning for us—for me and Devon. And I am not giving this guy back to Liz. No way, no how.*

"It looks like we're early," Elizabeth told Todd as they strolled arm in arm up the flower-lined walkway to the entrance of the country club.

"Yeah, the parking lot's still empty. Except for the caterers and staff," Todd added.

"They really did it up big for us," Elizabeth commented. Spotlights highlighted the gray stucco structure, and a red-and-white banner welcoming the students to the Sweet Valley High School prom waved in the evening breeze.

Elizabeth could almost smell the sweet scent of anticipation that filled the air, and a surge of excitement skated up her arms. In a few minutes the entire place would light up with music, activity, voices, and couples dancing and sharing their special night together. All their work and planning on the prom committees would soon pay off.

"Let's check to make sure all the details are worked out and everything's running smoothly, then maybe we can steal a private dance before the rest of the crew arrives," Todd suggested, leading her into the dimly lit entranceway.

"You know, you really shouldn't have lied to Courtney, telling her you weren't coming to the prom at all," Elizabeth admonished.

Todd shrugged. "It's better this way. If Courtney finds out I chose you over her *again,* it would only make things worse."

"I guess you're right about that," Elizabeth said quietly. "But I really don't want her to be hurt." She knew Courtney had a thing for Todd. She'd been after him for months. Todd had dated Courtney twice before, but both times he'd dumped Courtney to get back together with Elizabeth. Elizabeth shuddered as she remembered how angry Courtney had been the last time.

Todd squeezed her hand, and she shrugged off the memory as they entered the elegant grand ballroom. Elizabeth noticed a few couples were already there, admiring the decorations and munching on vegetables and dip. The tables looked stunning, draped with white linen table-cloths and filled with silver trays and fancy appetizers. In the center of each table crystal flower vases overflowed with red roses. Punch bowls were filled with bright fruit punch and sparkling cider, and tables full of sodas were situated in the corners of the room for easy accessibility. Twinkling lights were strung around the doorways and stage area where the DJ worked. The atmosphere looked elegant and sophisticated—just the image they'd wanted to create.

"The old-fashioned theme was a perfect idea, Todd," Elizabeth said sincerely. "I'm so glad you suggested it. It was like you read my mind."

"You know what they say—great minds think alike." Todd gave her a tender smile and brushed his finger over her cheek. "Maybe it was meant to be, for us to be here together tonight. Just like I'd always imagined."

"To end our junior year together." Elizabeth smiled, feeling the hint of tears prick her eyes as Todd brushed a soft kiss across her lips. When he pulled away, he was smiling wickedly. She grinned and pointed to the skyline the art students had painted along the wall, hoping to divert his attention and get her emotions under control. "The backdrop is fantastic. I love the decorations." Silver Mylar stars sparkled and glowed all around them, and the candlelight and soft background music created the perfect fantasy room for dancing and romance. Elizabeth felt as if she'd just stepped into a Fred Astaire and Ginger Rogers movie.

"It looks like the buffet is set up too," Todd said. "I can't wait to see if all that food tastes as good as it looks."

Elizabeth nodded. "Everything's in place. Even the DJ."

A tall, white-haired man wearing a starched white uniform with shiny brass buttons passed by. "That's the captain we hired for the yacht." Todd hurried over and stopped him. "Excuse me, Captain Adams. I'm Todd Wilkins."

The gentleman faced them, giving Elizabeth an appreciative look. He shook Todd's hand. "Yes, nice to see you again, Mr. Wilkins. You're the young man who organized this shindig."

Todd introduced Elizabeth. "Liz and I both worked on the prom committee. Liz is really the one responsible for making this night a success."

Elizabeth blushed. "Actually we have several committees. I can't take all the credit. Everyone worked hard."

The captain chuckled. "It looks as if your planning paid off. You should give yourselves a pat on the back." He glanced at Elizabeth's dress. "And you look lovely, Ms. Wakefield."

"She does, doesn't she?" Todd beamed proudly and curved his arm possessively around her waist. "Captain, we wanted to make sure everything was all set for after the dance."

The captain saluted him. "Yes, sir. The ship has been prepared and the staff appropriately fore-warned that a multitude of teens will be on board for the evening." Elizabeth giggled at the merry twinkle in the captain's gray eyes.

"Great." Todd shook the captain's hand and thanked him. "There shouldn't be any problems, then."

"I don't foresee any. The ship has been fully equipped and checked over in detail by my crew. We're scheduled to take off directly following your dance. Let me know if I can be of further assis-tance," the captain said with another salute. "For now, I think I shall go sit someplace quiet before the action descends." He made a dramatic gesture of rubbing his temple as if he were already getting a headache, and Elizabeth laughed again. "You two make a lovely couple. Enjoy your evening."

"It's going in our memory book," Elizabeth said, hugging closer to Todd.

"That's right." Todd swept her into his arms, twirled her around, then dipped her slightly back-ward. "And now, my fair lady, how about we sneak in a private dance before everyone else gets here?"

"I would love to," Elizabeth said, mimicking his playful tone.

Todd wrapped his arms around her, and they glided smoothly across the floor as if they were on-stage dancing for an audience. "Do you remember the first dance we went to together?" Todd asked, suddenly serious, searching deep into her eyes.

"Yes," Elizabeth said softly. "I had to wear a Band-Aid on each toe for two days after that."

Todd chuckled. "I was so nervous about dancing with you. I think I'd been in love with you since grade school."

"I was nervous too," Elizabeth admitted. "You were the first boy I ever kissed."

"I know." Todd wagged his eyebrows. "You almost bit my lip off."

Elizabeth whacked him on the arm. "I did not!"

Todd rubbed his lower lip with his hand and grinned wickedly. "It's OK. I didn't mind. I figure it was a battle scar well earned."

Elizabeth giggled, then raised her finger and rubbed the spot he had just touched. Todd's eyes grew serious, and he brushed his hand down Elizabeth's waist, pulling her closer. "I knew then you were the girl for me."

"Todd, let's just enjoy the night," Elizabeth said, remembering Devon. She'd called him from Todd's cell phone as well, but there was no answer at his house. Where could Devon be?

Todd nodded, then rubbed his hand over her bare back. "That dress is absolutely gorgeous, Liz. You're going to be the sexiest, most beautiful girl here tonight."

Elizabeth swallowed against the emotions suddenly swelling within her. Her heartbeat raced furiously, and she momentarily forgot they weren't alone. Todd's dark eyes mesmerized her.

"Those sequins sparkle just like your eyes, just like your face when you smile," Todd said in a husky voice.

The dim lights on the dance floor scattered slivers of soft light that flickered off the silver stars, and the few couples there disappeared into the scenery as Elizabeth got caught up in the romance and the heat of the moment. Todd was staring at her as if she were the only girl in the world. It felt so right to be in his arms, his warm breath fanning her cheek. In the background a female vocalist sang of love and finding the right man, and Elizabeth tightened her arms around Todd, wondering if she'd had the right man all along and hadn't known it.

"Elizabeth—"

A sudden commotion startled them both as a loud female yelp broke through the soft music, pelting through the room like jagged shards of glass. Todd frowned in confusion, and Elizabeth turned to see what was going on.

Courtney Kane was standing in the doorway with Lila, Jessica, and . . . Devon?

"Uh-oh," Todd mumbled.

Elizabeth froze, her breath catching in her throat. Courtney was glaring at her, her hands fisted by her sides, her face flaming. Devon's mouth gaped open, and Jessica and Lila both looked as if their eyes were about to pop out of their heads.

"I can't take this anymore!" Courtney shrieked. For an instant Elizabeth was sure Courtney was going to run across the room and attack her, but then the she devil turned and stormed out of the ballroom.

"Whew, Courtney's upset," Todd muttered darkly, tightening his arm around Elizabeth.

Who cares about Courtney? Elizabeth thought, her nerves coiling. *What is Jessica doing with Devon?*

Chapter 6

Jessica, Devon, and Lila screeched to a halt in the doorway just as Courtney stalked out in a blaze of red. But Jessica didn't care about Courtney. Elizabeth was staring straight at Devon. Jessica couldn't lose Devon now, not after they'd been so cozy on the ride over! Devon was finally warming up to her. She was working her charms on him, and in a matter of hours he'd be totally in love with her. He'd forget about her twin and be hers.

Elizabeth gave Jessica a shocked, wide-eyed look, and her heart suddenly did a crazy pitter-pat routine in her chest. She quickly glanced at Devon to see if he'd caught on yet, but he was watching Courtney as she retreated outside, stumbling and fussing in her black spiked heels. Thank goodness! He hadn't seen Elizabeth's reaction yet.

"I'll be right back, Devon," Jessica whispered.

She rushed across the dance floor as gracefully as possible in her high heels, grabbed her sister's hand, and pulled her out the back door toward the pool, ignoring Elizabeth's feeble protests.

"Jessica, what's going on?" Elizabeth demanded, trying to fight her sister's grasp as Jessica yanked on her arm.

"Shhh!" Jessica begged. "I need to talk to you."

"No kidding," Elizabeth said sharply, digging her heels into the polished floor.

"We have to go someplace quiet to talk," Jessica hissed.

Elizabeth finally relented, and Jessica dragged her out the French doors past the beautiful Olympic pool, where the smell of chlorine and fresh flowers filled the air. Japanese lanterns were hanging strategically around the dimly lit pool area, where tables were draped in mauve tablecloths and filled with snacks and more drinks—an outdoor extension to the cozy atmosphere of the ballroom.

Jessica practically pushed Elizabeth inside the pool room. "In here, Liz." As soon as they were inside she peeked out the doorway to make sure they hadn't been followed, then closed the door, her nerves grating as the metal hinges squeaked shut. She finally turned to face her sister. Elizabeth stood stock-still, her nostrils flared, her arms folded across her chest. She tapped her toe impatiently and looked like she was about to explode.

"Jessica Wakefield, what's going on? Why are *you* here with Devon?"

Jessica winced at Elizabeth's angry voice. Her twin sounded almost hysterical.

"Jess? Out with it—*now!*" Elizabeth demanded.

Jessica touched Elizabeth's arm in what she hoped was a soothing gesture. She couldn't be sure since her palms were sweating profusely. "Just calm down, Liz. I can explain everything. It's really a silly mistake."

Elizabeth's mouth tightened into a furious line. "Your explanation better not be silly. It had better be *good.*"

"It's like this. I . . . uh . . ." Jessica fumbled for an answer, her mind reeling. She had to think fast, or she'd lose Devon for good. *Oh, well, might as well go with the truth—at least most of it.* "I—"

"I thought I'd been stood up, and you show up here with *my* prom date!" Elizabeth fumed. "What did you do, kidnap him? I knew you wanted Devon, but I never thought you'd stoop to this."

"It's not like that at all," Jessica protested. A nervous laugh escaped her, but Elizabeth narrowed her eyes to slits, so Jessica bit back the laugh and cleared her throat. "OK, OK, don't lose your cool. I've fixed everything. It's all going to work out just fine."

Elizabeth arched both eyebrows and took a menacing step toward her. Jessica shrank back. "OK, here goes. This afternoon when Lila and I were out by the pool putting the finishing touches on our tans, Devon called and left this message. Only I forgot about it because I got another call from Jordan, and he'd changed his mind and had car trouble and wanted me to come to his house—"

"Jessica, get to the point," Elizabeth said, tapping her foot again, even more impatiently than before.

Jessica took a quick breath and forged on. "Well, Lila was there, and I was trying to keep my date a secret from her, so I completely forgot all about Devon's message."

"Which was?" Elizabeth said through gritted teeth.

"That you were supposed to meet him at Palomar House instead of Secca Lake." Jessica winced, waiting for the wrath of the twin.

"You conveniently forgot to tell me that! How rich!" Elizabeth got right in Jessica's face. "I can't believe you let me go to the lake all dressed up in my evening gown and sit there like an idiot, alone, thinking Devon didn't want to be with me—"

"But don't you see?" Jessica interrupted. "Later when Jordan dumped me, it was so traumatic—"

"Your date dumped you?" Elizabeth threw her hands in the air.

"It's a long story, and it's all Lila's fault," Jessica said, waving off the explanation. "Anyway, it's not important. But that's when I remembered about Devon's phone call. So I rushed over to Palomar

House and pretended to be you so Devon wouldn't think he'd been stood up. See, I did you a favor!"

"You did what?" Elizabeth stared at Jessica, obviously horrified. "Why did you pretend to be me? Why didn't you just tell him the truth—that you're such a ditz you forgot to give me the message? I was sitting at the lake for over an hour, completely miserable, wondering why Devon didn't show."

"You have to understand, Liz," Jessica pleaded. "I was so distraught over what happened with Jordan, and my night was totally ruined. And then I was mad at Lila, and Lila was mad at me, and we got in a big fight—"

Elizabeth snorted in disgust. "This is ridiculous! Why was Lila mad at you?"

Jessica folded her arms, then rapped her long fingernails up and down on her arm in a nervous gesture. "That's not important either. The point is, I didn't want anyone else being mad at me, so that's why I pretended to be you."

"What about now? *I'm* mad at you, Jess, or hasn't that sunk in? You've ruined my whole evening!" Elizabeth started pacing the length of the small room again, her breath coming in short, angry spurts. Jessica was afraid she was going to hyperventilate.

She had to think quickly, or everything was going to blow up. Todd's face flashed into her mind. Elizabeth had been dancing with Todd when they'd barged in. Jessica wasn't sure how her sister and Todd had ended up here together, but she knew she'd have to play the Todd card. "Liz, I know you're upset about Devon. But when I came in, you were dancing with Todd. And you had this dreamy look on your face." She softened her voice, hoping to play on her twin's sentimental side. "You looked pretty happy too, being with Todd. Maybe I did the right thing."

Elizabeth paused and stared at her, her expression changing from anger to disbelief, then filling with turmoil. Jessica could tell the wheels were turning in her sister's overanalytical brain and held her breath.

"I was having fun." Elizabeth's face crumpled. She sounded suspiciously close to tears. "What's wrong with me, Jess? I love being here with Todd, but I still want to be with Devon. I'm such a bad person! Why do I want them both?"

Jessica actually felt sorry for her sister. Elizabeth was usually so practical and levelheaded, but Jessica understood what it was like to be in love with more than one guy. She'd gone through the same thing a while back with Ken Matthews and Christian Gorman. Choosing between them had been heart wrenching. And Devon, what a temptation!

But then she remembered she was dateless and she wanted Devon for herself. It wasn't fair for Elizabeth to have both guys, at least not on prom night. She snapped her fingers, struck with a brilliant idea. "I know, Liz. I had a brainstorm! You can have what you want without hurting either guy."

Her twin arched a golden eyebrow, a seed of hope simmering in her blue-green eyes. Jessica smiled mischievously, liking her plan more and more. Actually it would solve *both* their problems.

"I know you're scheming again," Elizabeth said, obviously unsure whether to trust her sister.

Jessica smiled confidently. "But this will work. And if you don't do it, you're going to have to go out there right now and choose between Todd and Devon." She pointed to the ballroom, where other classmates had started to gather. "Which one of them do you want to hurt, Lizzie?"

"I don't want to hurt either of them," Elizabeth said in a small voice.

"Exactly." Jessica snapped her fingers. "And with my plan you won't."

Elizabeth nervously fidgeted with her watch. "OK. What's your idea?" she finally asked.

Jessica threw her arm around Elizabeth's shoulders. "It's the perfect solution, Liz. I'll stay by Devon's side all night pretending to be you, and you can enjoy being with Todd at the prom. That way no one gets hurt, and it'll buy you more time to make up your mind."

Elizabeth looked like someone had just presented her with a two-page-long word problem—totally baffled.

"So?" Jessica prodded. "What do you think?"

"You want to stay with Devon and pretend to

91

be me? How can that possibly be the perfect solution?" Elizabeth couldn't believe her ears. Jessica had always been a little off, but this time she'd completely lost her mind.

Jessica grabbed her hand and sat her down, obviously in prime scheming mode. "Well, you said you wanted both of them. If we switch tonight, you'll get to have your special prom night with Todd, and he won't be hurt. And Devon will never be the wiser." There was an excited spark in Jessica's eyes. "And when the night is over, you can still have Devon for the rest of the weekend. That way you'll get to have both of them!"

Elizabeth bit down on her tongue as she mulled over the idea. Jessica's face glowed with the brilliance of her plan, and the more Elizabeth thought about it . . .

A rap song ended, and they heard laughter from inside the ballroom. Elizabeth craned her neck and heard the DJ announce he was going to play some serious dance music. Todd would probably come looking for her any minute. She had to decide something soon.

"But let's start off with a favorite oldie," the DJ interjected. Seconds later a Beach Boys tune wafted from the inside, and Jessica sighed impatiently. Todd and Devon were both in the ballroom. What if they'd already discovered the truth?

The thought of leaving Todd for the night broke her heart. He'd been so sweet all evening, reminding her of all the wonderful memories they shared. He'd gone to the lake because he was missing her, and he looked so great, and he'd been so romantic all night. And even after all that had happened lately, he'd dumped Courtney to escort her.

But she remembered the sweet things Devon had said the night he'd asked her to the prom. Plus Jessica really wanted Devon for herself. The idea of Jessica flirting with Devon all night—even if she was pretending to be Elizabeth—didn't sit well. The last time they'd switched on Devon, he'd been angry and hurt. Their switch had blown up in their faces, and she'd almost lost Devon for good.

What was she going to do?

"Come on, Liz. It's the best way," Jessica urged. "Both guys are totally cool. And you know you don't want to hurt Todd or Devon, especially tonight." Jessica shot a nervous look toward the country club. Elizabeth followed her gaze and saw Todd step out onto the patio. He scanned the area as if he was searching for her. Courtney had already left, so if Elizabeth deserted Todd, he'd be alone. She couldn't do that to him.

"But Jess, there's still one problem. Remember the last time you tried to fool Devon? It didn't work."

Jessica shrugged. "I *did* fool him for a while. He only figured it out when we kissed." Jessica's cheeks turned crimson. She immediately averted her gaze as if she wished she hadn't mentioned kissing.

Elizabeth frowned, realizing that Jessica must have already kissed Devon tonight. She glared at her sister, but out of the corner of her eye she caught a glimpse of Todd strolling around the pool. He was definitely looking for her.

"OK, Jess, I'll do it. But I don't want to hear about you kissing him," Elizabeth snapped. She pointed her finger at Jessica. "And no more kissing is allowed tonight, do you understand me?"

Jessica hesitated, and Elizabeth spotted a devilish gleam in her twin's eyes. She saw Todd step back inside, looking perplexed.

"I mean it, Jess," she said in a hard voice. "It could ruin the whole plan."

"All right, all right," Jessica agreed grudgingly. "No more kissing!"

Elizabeth took a deep breath and smoothed down her dress. Jessica fluffed her hair with her hands. "Let's go," Elizabeth said, glancing nervously at the ballroom, where other kids mingled and converged on the snacks. She shivered as the cool evening breeze brushed her cheeks. Or maybe it was from the fear ballooning in her stomach.

"We might just pull this off," she said, pressing a hand to her forehead. She gave Jessica a sharp look and opened the door. "As long as we keep Todd and Devon away from each other."

Lila struggled to keep Devon's attention so he wouldn't go looking for Elizabeth. As soon as

Jessica had grabbed her twin's hand Lila had noticed Devon start to follow. If he caught up with her and saw the twins together, the whole night would turn into a disaster. Not that it could get much worse, but she wished Jessica would hurry up and give Devon back to Elizabeth so Lila would have someone to hang out with.

Of course, this date sitting wasn't so terrible. Devon was absolutely gorgeous. She'd thought he was just some guy on a motorcycle Jessica temporarily had the hots for, but up close and personal, he oozed sex appeal. Hmmm . . . Jessica mentioned date stealing, and so far no one else's date even looked appealing. *Maybe if Elizabeth and Jessica kill each other in the pool house, I can snag Devon for my own.*

"Wonder when Liz is coming back," Devon said. Ice clinked in his glass as he sipped his soda.

Lila laughed softly. "Oh, you know girls. They're probably in the powder room, and Jessica is talking her head off." She gave Devon one of her best sultry smiles. "The decorations look fantastic, don't they?"

"Yeah, it came out pretty cool," Devon said, his slate blue eyes scrutinizing the room appreciatively. Lila noticed some of the other kids arriving from her party.

"OK, guys, let's get down to some good old rock and roll," the DJ said in a smooth voice. The music piped up, and noisy, excited chatter filled the room. Couples meandered to the dance floor hand in hand, and the lights dimmed to a golden glow illuminating the room.

"I heard you helped too," Lila said, gently placing her hand on Devon's arm. She raked her gaze over him and winked. "Just what hidden talents do you have, Devon Whitelaw?"

"No special talents, really." Devon shrugged, then glanced down into her eyes and smiled. "But working on the committee was a lot more fun than I thought it would be. I guess everyone's excitement kind of rubbed off on me." He ran his hand through his hair, and Lila noticed a loose strand tumble down over his forehead. He looked incredible in his white jacket and shirt, sophisticated and mature. And the serious expression in his eyes made him seem older than the other junior guys, almost as if he were old enough to be in college. Hmmm, he was looking more appealing all the time.

"I'm looking forward to the cruise after the dance," Lila said. "It should be romantic—all that moonlight on the water."

Devon nodded. "It was nice of your folks to let everyone come over earlier. Where's your date, Lila?"

"Uh, he's meeting me later," Lila improvised. *As soon as I steal him from someone else,* she amended silently, glancing around the room for a possibility.

"He'd better hurry, or all the good food will be gone," Devon said.

Lila laughed. "Oh, I'm not worried about that." She lowered her dark lashes, watching as Devon followed the movement. She was glad she'd chosen the low-cut black dress and knew it hugged her curves in all the right places. A guy had to notice, and finally Devon had stopped searching the room for the wonder twin and was starting to pay attention. In a few more minutes she'd have him totally captivated.

Suddenly Jessica seemed to appear out of nowhere. "Oh, there you are, Devon." She slid her hand under Devon's arm possessively and smiled up at him.

Lila stiffened when Devon immediately turned to Jessica. "Liz, I was wondering when you were coming back," Lila said through clenched teeth.

"I'm here now," Jessica clipped, giving Lila a quick warning glance behind Devon's back. Then she rubbed her finger over Devon's arm. "And I'm not leaving your side all night, Devon."

Devon squared his shoulders, looking proud. His eyes twinkled with pleasure. "That sounds good to me."

"And the next song is for all those lovers," the DJ announced softly. A slow ballad began.

Jessica tugged on Devon's arm. "Come on, let's go dance." Jessica shot Lila a practiced smile. "Thanks for date sitting, Lila."

Lila glanced over Devon's shoulder and saw Elizabeth enter through the rear door and join Todd. Elizabeth had a wary expression in her eyes, but Todd didn't seem to notice. Lila grabbed Jessica's hand. "Excuse us just a minute, Devon. I have to ask *Elizabeth* something really important."

Jessica tensed, obviously irritated, but Lila didn't care. Her friend owed her an explanation.

"Be right back," Jessica mumbled as Lila pulled her away.

"What's going on, Jess?" Lila hissed, leaning in close. "I thought you were going to ditch Devon when you got here and we were going to hang out together."

"Change of plans," Jessica replied lightly. "There was a terrible mix-up, and guess what? I'm filling in for Liz for the whole night."

"What?" Lila's voice raised to a near shriek.

"Well, you see, Todd showed up at the lake, and you know Liz. She doesn't want to hurt anyone's feelings." Jessica giggled. "But I don't have time to explain now. Devon's waiting!"

"But Jessica—"

"I'm getting him for the whole night!" Jessica laughed excitedly. "Isn't it wonderful?"

Lila stood in stunned silence as Jessica turned and sauntered away. Then she saw Elizabeth cuddle in Todd's embrace, gliding to the soft music. Ken and Olivia, Winston and Maria, even Enid and Blubber filed onto the dance floor. Then the DJ played a popular dance tune, picking up the pace.

Lila clenched her hands into fists as Jessica took Devon's arm and led him onto the dance floor as if she had everything under control. Lila couldn't believe it. Jessica had spoiled her date with Jordan, forgotten to give her sister a message about her date, fooled Devon by playing Elizabeth, and still wound up with a great guy. Fuming, Lila headed to the punch table to get a glass of something cold to douse her boiling temper.

Once again the Wakefield twins both had their men and everything turned out rosy for them. But she was left out in the cold—not only dateless but *friendless* on the biggest night of the school year. She twisted her purse string into a knot. She had never been this mad at Jessica in her whole life!

Chapter 7

Devon curved his arm around Elizabeth, enjoying the way her lithe body was pressed securely against his as they swayed to the soft beat of the music floating through the room. He'd been concentrating so hard on not stepping on Elizabeth's toes, he'd barely been able to talk. Now he relaxed and inhaled the fresh, sweet scent of her shampoo and a perfume that smelled of gardenias. Hmmm, she usually smelled like roses. Maybe she'd worn a new fragrance for the special night. Whatever the explanation, he loved the new scent. It was sweet and enticing at the same time.

Other couples danced around them, laughter and voices filling the crowded dance floor. A.J. and Aaron Dallas were comically waltzing together as their dates looked on and laughed. Enid and Blubber danced by, and Blubber stepped on Enid's tiny foot. Devon winced, but Enid just bit her lip and forced a smile. Devon was pleased to see she seemed to be relaxing a bit.

"It looks like Enid is warming up to Blubber," Devon commented.

"Good for her," Elizabeth said without much interest. Devon frowned. It was really odd that Elizabeth was being so cold. Something just didn't feel right. He glanced over his shoulder at Jessica for the zillionth time, checking her out. What was she doing with Wilkins? And why did Todd's date arrive all dressed up, then freak and leave?

Elizabeth lifted her head off his shoulder and glanced up at him, and he pulled back slightly to look into her bright blue-green eyes. She looked like a goddess in that slinky white dress, and for a minute he forgot what he was going to say. Then he glimpsed Jessica's shimmering lavender gown again and remembered. "Liz, what's Jessica doing with Todd?"

Elizabeth nibbled on her bottom lip a minute, and Devon tensed, wondering if he shouldn't have asked. He didn't want to remind her of Todd if it upset her, especially since tonight was the beginning of what he hoped was a long romance between *him* and Elizabeth.

Then Elizabeth trailed a finger down the outside of his arm and moved closer to him. "I guess I never mentioned it, Devon," she said softly, "but Jessica and Todd have a history together."

Devon's step faltered, and he almost tripped over his own feet. He caught himself at the last moment and simply stared at her in shock. "Are you kidding? I thought you and Todd had been together for a long time."

Elizabeth shrugged, loosening her arms around his neck and focusing on some obscure spot on his shirt. "We were, but I always suspected Jessica and Todd had a thing for each other."

Devon was baffled. "I can't believe how conniving Jessica is," he said, glancing over Elizabeth's bare shoulder at her sneaky twin and wondering how Elizabeth could be so tolerant. "How could she do that to you—her own sister?" He grimaced, feeling protective over Elizabeth. "Doesn't Jessica care about anyone but herself?"

Suddenly Elizabeth froze in his arms, her beautiful lips tightening into a frown. "Don't talk about Jessica that way, Devon. She's not as selfish as you think." She clenched her hands into balls and rested them on his shoulders. For a minute he thought she was going to bolt away from him, and his heart pounded in panic. Then she continued in a softer, affectionate voice. "She's the best sister in the world."

At Elizabeth's tone Devon swallowed anything he might have wanted to say and backed off. Obviously this was a sore subject for Elizabeth. Jessica must have hurt her before, but Elizabeth was so nice, she still stood up for her sister. He guessed they shared that special twin bond or something, but Devon still thought families and siblings should take care of each other, not play dirty tricks behind each other's backs.

He was only angry because he cared so much about Elizabeth, not because he minded Jessica being with Todd. In fact, if Jessica and Todd got together, Devon wouldn't have any competition for Elizabeth's heart.

The slow song ended, and some couples left the dance floor as a fast techno song blasted through the speakers. Devon expected Elizabeth to beg off the next dance, but she simply grinned and moved out of his embrace. Maria Slater and Tyler took center stage as they displayed some complex moves.

Devon watched Elizabeth, determined to savor every minute with her. "I'm sorry, Liz. I didn't mean to upset you by talking about Jessica and Todd." He threaded his fingers through hers, clasping their joined hands against his side. "I promise I won't mention them again."

Elizabeth looked up and gave him a radiant smile, then squeezed his hand and began to dance to the driving beat. "You're right. This is our night together. So let's forget about them and party!"

Devon nodded. He was a little surprised at Elizabeth's swift mood change but shrugged it off. Maybe she really was getting over Wilkins. Devon was fascinated by the graceful way she swayed and turned.

He always imagined she was a good dancer, but he never thought she would be so free and uninhibited.

"You're beautiful!" Devon shouted over the driving beat.

"What?" Elizabeth replied.

"I said, you're beautiful!" Devon yelled out just as the song hit a quieter part. His voice resonated through the crowded ballroom. A bunch of kids turned to stare, and a few of them laughed. Devon felt his cheeks turn bright red. He saw Jessica gaping at him from across the dance floor, her face as white as a sheet. It seemed an odd reaction, but then, this was turning out to be kind of an odd night.

"You're so sweet, Devon," Elizabeth said, wrapping her arms around his neck. "Nothing like a public declaration to make a girl's night."

Devon regained his composure and circled her waist with his arms. "I'll do it again if you want," he said playfully.

Elizabeth just smiled and rested her cheek on his chest.

Devon loved the feel of Elizabeth in his arms. She was so soft and natural and—

Something caught Devon's eye, and he looked up to find Jessica and Todd dancing nearby. He narrowed his eyes, an odd feeling skittering through him as he zeroed in on Jessica's face. She looked incredibly beautiful tonight. Less made up and overtly sexy than usual. And there was something about the way she was looking at Todd—

"I wish this night would never end," Elizabeth murmured, gazing up at him. All thoughts of Jessica and Todd were instantaneously erased. Devon had more important things to focus on—like Elizabeth.

Elizabeth was still reeling over Devon's little flattery-of-Jessica outburst as she and Todd danced to the romantic ballad. *He thought he was talking to you,* Elizabeth reminded herself. But then the doubts started to filter through. What if Jessica was letting a little bit of Jessica show through and Devon was attracted to it? What if he preferred her sister?

When the song ended, Elizabeth pulled away from Todd, feeling a bit worn out. Then the beat changed to a funky rap song, and she was excited when Todd motioned to the food tables. "I need some fuel."

"I'm hungry too," Elizabeth said, remembering she'd missed dinner. She followed Todd to the buffet, and they filled their plates. The caterers had served everything from dip and chips to miniature sandwiches and desserts to small crab quiches. Enid came up behind Elizabeth, giving her dress a puzzled look and glancing at Todd in confusion. Elizabeth knew her best friend was wondering why she'd changed dresses and how she'd ended up with Todd. Elizabeth was beginning to wonder about that second part herself.

"I'll explain later," she whispered. "How are you getting along with Tad?"

Enid shrugged and heaped food on her plate. "OK, I guess. At least he hasn't been talking football plays all night. But if he steps on my foot one more time, I'm going to be on crutches for the rest of the weekend."

Elizabeth laughed. "Maybe you should have worn steel-toed shoes."

Enid giggled. "I've never seen anyone eat as much as he can either."

Todd maneuvered between them and grabbed some more shrimp. "Hey, I could eat two pounds of this stuff myself," Todd said, stuffing one into his mouth.

The girls laughed, then Elizabeth nodded toward the door. "Let's go out by the gazebo and make a picnic," Elizabeth suggested. She felt an intense need to get out of the ballroom. She was sick of watching Jessica shamelessly flirt with Devon. Plus she'd noticed Devon repeatedly glancing her way. It was all so nerve-racking, and she wanted to be able to focus on Todd. He was being so wonderful.

"The gazebo sounds great to me," Todd said, juggling a glass of punch along with his overloaded plate. He bit off a piece of celery and followed Elizabeth outside. "Feels good out here. I was getting hot dancing."

He wiggled his eyebrows, and Elizabeth giggled. It was time to put Devon and Jessica out of her thoughts. She'd made a decision to stay with Todd, and she was going to stick with it.

"Better not complain, or I'll drag you back in there," Elizabeth threatened. "The night is only beginning."

Todd stopped, then leaned forward to nuzzle Elizabeth's neck. "Hey, who's complaining? I like holding you in my arms." Elizabeth rushed forward playfully, laughing as he hurried to catch up with her.

"Behave yourself, Wilkins," Elizabeth whispered as they bypassed several couples stepping outside for fresh air. "People are watching."

Todd grinned and glanced at a few guys and their dates relaxing on the patio furniture. "Well, if anyone's watching, they're jealous." His eyes grew serious. "Because they know I'm with the prettiest girl at Sweet Valley High."

A tingle of delight tickled Elizabeth's insides. Todd was an angel. He was attentive, charming, and funny, and being with him felt right. She hadn't had this much fun with him in ages.

"Come on, let's go into my private abode," Todd said in a deep voice, gesturing toward the ivy-covered gazebo.

Elizabeth ducked and walked inside, settling onto one of the long wooden benches. Todd joined her, sitting so close, his knee brushed hers. "You know, I don't get it, Liz. What happened with Jessica? Why is she with Devon?"

Elizabeth froze, a cracker poised close to her mouth. She couldn't tell Todd the truth, obviously.

But she hated lying to him. "You know Jessica had a thing for Devon from the start," she began. "I guess he decided he liked Jessica better." She stared at the ground, wondering if her words were actually true and unable to look at Todd for fear he'd see the guilt in her eyes.

"I can't believe Devon and Jess would do that to you, Liz," Todd said, sounding shocked. "Devon must be a real idiot."

Elizabeth felt even worse because Todd was angry for her. "I really don't want to talk about them. OK?"

Todd nodded and gave her an understanding smile. Elizabeth chewed on a celery stick, her appetite dwindling.

"Sure, whatever you say, Liz. I'm just glad we wound up together."

"What about Courtney?" Elizabeth asked, remembering the way she had stormed out of the country club earlier. Elizabeth was surprised she hadn't confronted them. Her normal style was to bulldoze over anyone who got in her way. "Did you go after her and try to explain?"

"Yeah, I went after her." Todd sighed. "But I couldn't find her anywhere. And I didn't see her car."

"I feel terrible," Elizabeth said, rolling a carrot stick in the dip. "I know what it's like to be stood up. Maybe you should have tried harder, Todd. I'm sure you could find her and make her understand what happened."

"I don't know. I think I should call her after she's cooled off," Todd replied. "I think then it'll be easier for her to understand." He tipped her chin up with his thumb. "Besides, right now I want to spend every minute I can with you."

Elizabeth's heart soared. Todd's brown eyes glowed with tenderness. A halo of moonlight silhouetted his handsome face, making him even more sexy. Being with Todd like this was the way she'd always dreamed prom night would be.

Elizabeth heard familiar laughter and looked up to find Maria, Tyler, Enid, Blubber, Olivia, and Ken emerging from the ballroom. Blubber carried two plates, one filled with appetizers and the other stacked with desserts, and Enid was sipping fruit punch from a plastic cup.

Elizabeth smiled when her eyes fell on Ken and Olivia. Ken's classic black tux offset Olivia's daring lime green dress perfectly. And Maria's date, Tyler, looked gorgeous in a navy tux jacket and black pants. As always, Maria's ebony skin glowed beautifully and she looked classy—her simple black strapless dress was complemented by a lacy silver shawl. Even Enid and Tad made a nice-looking couple. Enid's emerald green dress with crisscross spaghetti straps showed off her petite figure and Tad had picked out an emerald bow tie and cumberbund to match.

"Hey, mind if we join you lovebirds?" Maria joked.

"Of course not," Elizabeth said, blushing. "I

was just thinking how sophisticated we all look tonight."

"I feel more comfortable in my football uniform," Tad joked.

Everyone laughed, settling in around Todd and Elizabeth. Todd gestured toward the ballroom. "It's a great party, isn't it?"

"Everything turned out just like we planned," Enid said. "Especially the decorations."

"I can't remember when I've danced so much," Maria said dreamily.

"Man, this girl here is wearing me out," Tyler said, giving Maria a teasing look. Maria beamed, and Elizabeth grinned at her friend, grateful her date was working out so well. It had been a long time since Maria had met a nice guy.

Maria scooted past Tyler to sit next to Elizabeth. "So? Give," she whispered. "What's up with you and bachelor number one?"

"I'll explain later," Elizabeth whispered.

Maria nodded, and Elizabeth noticed Enid was sitting with her back rigid, looking decidedly less than comfortable. She hoped her friend relaxed soon and had a good time.

"Are you guys ready for the Battle of the Junior Classes?" Todd asked. Every year all the schools in the area threw a giant fair on prom weekend. One of the events was a competition between all the junior classes—kind of a way to get them psyched for senior year. But the nature

111

of the competition was never announced until first thing Saturday morning.

"I'm always ready, as long as it's sports," Ken said. Tad seconded the opinion.

"That would be a disaster," Olivia said. "If it's a sports event, Sweet Valley will crash and burn with me as your captain."

"You'll be the perfect leader no matter what," Ken said, touching Olivia's nose. Olivia had been elected captain of the Sweet Valley High team earlier that week. Elizabeth knew her friend was honored by the distinction.

"Well, we'll find out tomorrow morning when I meet with the other captains," Olivia said. "I can't wait to get started."

"I hope it's a tennis tournament," Elizabeth said.

"Maybe it's a marathon day of different sports," Tad suggested.

"Or an arts show," Olivia said.

The guys groaned.

"Maybe it's going to be a dance contest," Enid suggested. "You know, whoever can stay on their feet longest wins?"

"I'd definitely win as long as I had Olivia as my partner," Ken declared.

Everyone moaned at Ken's sappiness, then they all started talking at once. Elizabeth glanced around at all her friends, ecstatic that her best friends and their dates were sharing this special night with her and Todd.

"Let's toast our junior year," Todd said, raising

his punch glass. "We're going out with a bang!" Everyone echoed the sentiment and clinked glasses. Ken and Olivia cuddled together, looking totally in love. Todd dropped a kiss on Elizabeth's cheek, and Elizabeth kissed him back, blushing more as Maria and Enid giggled at her.

She relaxed and nestled against Todd, relieved that everything was turning out fine. Tonight would truly be a night for her scrapbook.

Courtney pushed a branch away from her face and leaned forward. She was hiding in a bush outside the country club, and the aggravating foliage was scratching at her bare arms. She grimaced when she noticed she'd chipped the red polish off the tip of her pinky. Her beautiful red dress had twigs and leaves clinging to it, and her Gucci heels were ruined in the soft dirt. A dank stench wafting from the woods behind her made her wonder if something lurked in the darkness, watching *her* as she watched the students at the prom. But she ignored the inconvenience, readjusted her position, and knelt behind the gazebo, listening to every word the Sweet Valley students said.

Especially Todd Wilkins and Elizabeth Wakefield. Courtney had thought it was Elizabeth with Devon at Lila's party, but it turned out Elizabeth had been here with Todd the entire time. Dumped for Elizabeth Wakefield *again!* Acid burned a hole in her stomach as she heard them mention her name. Then Todd brushed her off completely.

Todd and Elizabeth were snuggling and laughing and talking with all their other friends while she hid like a criminal in the filthy bushes—and she hadn't even done anything wrong! Her fingernails dug into the painted wood at the base of the gazebo, and she felt paint peel and curl underneath her fingers. She completely forgot about her nail polish and almost drew blood.

"We're going to dance the night away," she heard Todd say.

"You're so romantic," Elizabeth replied with a silly giggle.

Courtney gritted her teeth at their sickening tone. Her whole body burned with fury as she recalled Todd's words. *I think I should call her after she's cooled off.*

Bile rose in her throat, and she swallowed. She crawled a safe distance away, then stood, fisting her hands by her sides. Yes, Courtney understood perfectly. Todd had asked her to the prom and used her to make that sappy Elizabeth Wakefield jealous, for the *third* time. She strode away from the gazebo, determined to make Todd and that wicked Wakefield twin pay. A plan quickly formed in her mind, and she tossed her mahogany hair over her shoulder.

Three times and you're out, buddy, Courtney thought, turning to fix Todd with an evil glare. *Better have fun while you can. 'Cause you're in for a big surprise.*

Chapter 8

Jessica was totally impressed by Devon's moves. He could definitely hold his own next to Aaron and A.J. and the rest of the jock boys, who hardly even moved their feet. Jessica noticed Suzanne Hanlon casting an envious glance her way, and she waved, moving closer to Devon just to show off.

Winston and Maria were doing some old-fashioned shag dance, and a whole crowd was watching and laughing as Winston twirled and bounced around. Some of the football players started a conga line. Amy Sutton grabbed the rest of the cheerleaders and joined on the end, laughing as the long line wove its way around the room.

Jessica couldn't have dreamed up a better prom. She was surrounded by all her friends, dancing with a gorgeous guy, and having the time of her life.

Grinning devilishly, Jessica bumped her hips against Devon's. He smiled and grabbed her wrist to twirl her around. When she stopped spinning, his eyes locked on hers, and Jessica could see the longing in their slate blue depths. She batted her long lashes at him and heard him catch his breath.

Devon wanted her. She knew it. They were really connecting. And even if he did think she was Elizabeth, this time Devon wouldn't be able to deny the connection between them. He brushed a strand of hair away from her cheek, and she shivered at his touch. Maybe later, if things went well, she'd reveal who she really was. Maybe Devon would finally be hers.

Jessica felt a sharp tug on her arm and turned to find Lila glaring at her. Jessica was not in the mood to deal with her best friend's moping problem. She quickly slipped from her friend's clutches, but Lila was persistent and grabbed her arm again, tugging harder. Jessica winced and noticed Lila's fingerprints embedded on her bronzed skin.

"What's going on?" Devon asked, obviously puzzled by Lila's bizarre behavior.

"Come on, I need to see you in the bathroom—*now*," Lila spat out.

"I'll be right back," Jessica whispered to Devon. "Lila needs to tell me something."

Devon nodded, his expression confused. "Sure, Liz. I'll get us some punch."

Jessica gritted her teeth and followed Lila into

the ladies' room. When she stepped inside the elegant rest room, she was grateful to note that the plush sitting area was vacant. Jessica spun around to face her friend and almost jumped back. Lila looked as if she was ready to explode.

"Why did you drag me in here?" Jessica asked, refusing to be intimidated.

"I needed to talk to you," Lila shot back.

"Why are you being such a party pooper, Li? This is prom night, and you're acting like a dragon queen!"

Lila's dark eyes glittered like two red sparks sizzling from an out-of-control fire. "I'm being what?" She jammed her hands on her hips and leaned toward Jessica, her nostrils flaring with anger. "How could you say that to me after the way you've been acting tonight?"

Jessica took a deep breath. "I'm just trying to have a good time with Devon," she said, maintaining her cool. "There's nothing wrong with that. But you have to stop coming up to me. Devon's not stupid. He knows you aren't friends with Liz." Her voice grew more agitated. "You're going to blow the whole night!"

"Well, this whole date-stealing idea isn't working out!" Lila snapped. "At least not for me! Penny's date won't even look at me, and I've been standing by the wall all night. People are starting to stare. And I swear Caroline Pearce is taking notes for the gossip line!"

Jessica folded her arms across her chest. "Well, just try harder or something," she prodded. "But leave me out of it. I have to concentrate on Devon."

"I can't believe how selfish you are." Lila's voice was nearing a shout. "You not only ruined my date with Jordan, but now you ditched me for your sister's man!"

"Give me a break," Jessica said sarcastically. "You're just as much to blame for us losing Jordan as I am. And now you're messing up my quality time with Devon." Jessica paced across the small room. "Look, Lila, I only have this one night to win him over before I have to give him back to Liz!"

Lila lifted her chin in the air. "Well, maybe I should just tell Devon what you and his precious little Elizabeth are up to."

Jessica's mouth fell open in shock. "You wouldn't do that." She swallowed, studying Lila, her heart racing. "And even if you did tell him, he'd never believe you."

"Oh, I think he would."

"Why would he trust a girl he hardly knows over dear sweet Liz?" Jessica asked. She was trying very hard to look carefree, but inside she was freaking. Lila was capable of blowing her out of the water, and they both knew it.

Lila snatched her small purse and growled. "Forget it! You're not worth the effort!" she sneered. "I can't even stand to be in the same room with you anymore." Lila clutched the sides of her satiny dress and barreled toward the door. "And thanks a lot for ruining my prom!" She stormed dramatically from the room, slamming the door behind her.

Jessica inhaled a shaky breath, trying to calm her nerves, then checked her appearance in the mirror. Her cheeks were flushed and her eyes sparkly from the heated confrontation. She did feel a little twinge about her best friend being stuck alone on such an important night, but Lila would have to understand that this was Jessica's big chance and she couldn't give it up. Taking a tissue from a silver box on the counter, she dabbed at the corners of her eyes to soften her makeup, then stepped back to make sure the lingering effects of her argument with Lila had disappeared. Suddenly she thought she heard a noise in the bathroom stall behind her. She pivoted and peeked around the door, craning to hear.

"Hello?" She paused, her nerves on edge. "Hello, anyone there?"

But no one answered. Only her own voice echoed from the bare walls. Jessica felt foolish. She had to get back to Devon. Like she'd told Lila, every minute counted, and she was determined to win Devon tonight. He was going to see how desirable Jessica Wakefield could be. And nothing was going to stop her.

*   *   *

Courtney couldn't believe her luck. She slipped out of the bathroom stall and looked into the mirror with a self-satisfied smirk. So, the Wakefield twins had pulled a switch. Sweeping her brush through the tangled strands of her hair, she giggled in delight. Wouldn't Todd and Devon be interested in hearing about *that*?

Stepping back, she admired her sensational figure and how the red sequined dress sparkled under the fluorescent lights. *Like a devil in disguise,* she thought with a wry laugh. *You guys haven't seen anything yet.*

Now for the rest of her plan. She snapped her black velvet purse closed, her mind spinning as she recalled the nasty episode between Lila and Jessica. Lila had been really upset when she'd left—so upset, she'd most likely be up for a little revenge. *What a lucky break for me!*

She tapped her fingernails on the porcelain counter, deep in thought. Maybe she could get Lila on her side—*if* she played her cards right. In fact, Lila might be more than happy to help her because her plan would not only break dear sweet Elizabeth's heart, it would teach that self-centered Jessica a much needed lesson. She twirled around, clicking her heels on the floor with confidence. And it would show Todd Wilkins not to mess with Courtney Kane, or he'd pay. Big time.

She opened the door and slipped out of the bathroom. Jessica was talking to two of the Sweet

Valley High cheerleaders a few feet away. *Better not let her see me,* Courtney thought. Ducking her head, she bolted for the dance floor, ready to set phase one of her plan in motion.

Look out, guys, here I come. The fun is just about to begin!

Devon loosened his tie slightly, grabbed a cup of the fruity red punch, and chugged it while Elizabeth was in the bathroom. So far the night had been a huge success. He'd held Elizabeth in his arms and danced with her all night—which was really all he wanted. But as an added bonus Elizabeth was totally flirting with him and she was definitely having a good time. After tonight, no more Todd Wilkins. Devon would be on her mind all the time. He pondered the idea of being part of a couple. Devon and Elizabeth. Elizabeth and Devon. It sounded pretty cool.

He heard cheering coming from the dance floor and turned around to check it out. A bunch of kids had formed a circle and were pumping their arms in the air as they took turns showcasing their moves in the center. At that moment Winston was gettin' down with both Marias and Amy Sutton. It was hilarious, but it struck Devon as odd that Jessica wasn't right in the middle. She usually had to be the center of attention. Not like his sweet Elizabeth.

Jessica was most likely off working her charms

on Wilkins somewhere. She probably wanted to get Todd alone so she could sink her claws in as deep as she could get them before the poor guy came to his senses.

He thought about Elizabeth and how she'd been laughing and dancing and cozying up to him all night. Surprisingly, she'd been a party animal. But it was nice. He was glad to know Elizabeth could let her hair down and have a good time.

Everything had been smooth, except he knew Elizabeth couldn't stand to see her old boyfriend and her twin sister together. He sighed, wishing Jessica and Todd could be a little more discreet about their feelings. Their blatant show of affection was obviously upsetting Elizabeth. Couldn't Jessica be just a little more considerate of her twin?

A flash of bright red caught his eye, and he saw Courtney Kane saunter into the room and look around. Devon was surprised she was still here but even more surprised when she turned and headed his way. Why wasn't she looking for Wilkins? Elizabeth had said the girl was dangerous, and after her earlier temper tantrum Devon believed it was possible. He squared his shoulders and stared at her evenly, wondering what she wanted with him.

"Hi, Devon." Courtney rubbed herself up against him, and he stiffened, pouring himself another cup of punch to occupy his hands. "Having fun?"

"Yeah," Devon said cautiously.

"Where's Jessica?" Courtney asked softly.

Devon shrugged. "I don't know; why would you ask me?"

Courtney's lashes fluttered down over her smoky eyes, and he realized she was flirting with him. He pulled back, automatically determined to resist her charms, but she leaned closer to him, so close he inhaled the strong scent of her cloying perfume, probably some French concoction that cost a fortune an ounce. He coughed and inched away.

"Well, you oughta know, Devon," Courtney said sweetly. "You've been dancing with her all night."

Devon froze, his breath locking in his chest.

"I thought you were coming with Liz, but I guess she and Todd got back together, huh?" Courtney continued.

"What are you talking about?" Devon's heart was pounding, and he struggled to control a gnawing dread that was starting to take over his heart.

"Well, haven't you seen Elizabeth and Todd? They've been all over each other tonight. That's the reason he stood me up." Courtney smiled serenely. "I mean, he must have had a good reason to ditch *me*, right?"

Devon searched the room for Elizabeth. It wasn't true, it couldn't be. . . .

"You and Jessica really do make quite a lovely couple," Courtney said with a laugh. She gave him a coy smile, then turned and walked off.

Devon stared after her for a moment, unsure of what to believe. Jessica had been with Todd all night. He hadn't even spoken to her—

A sliver of fear wound up his spine. Jessica and Elizabeth hadn't pulled another switch on him again, had they? He wiped a bead of perspiration from his forehead and thought back over the evening. If they had switched, it would explain why Elizabeth had been hanging out with cheerleaders at Lila's party and dancing like crazy all night. Her overexuberance at everything, the different perfume . . . Enid's strange looks . . .

Laughter erupted from across the room, and Devon glanced up, thinking he heard Elizabeth. But Jessica and Todd were coming through the back door with Maria, Olivia, Enid, and their dates. Todd had his arm draped around Jessica's shoulders, and Jessica was laughing at something Maria said. Suddenly reality rushed in on Devon, and his fingers tightened around his punch glass. He felt like throwing it on the floor and watching it smash into pieces. Jessica hanging out with Maria and Olivia? Elizabeth going to the rest room with Lila? He swallowed, a sick feeling rising all the way from the pit of his stomach to his throat.

Courtney was right. Fury hit him, hard and swift. Elizabeth and Jessica had tricked him again!

Hurt and anger beat a fast rhythm through Devon's chest, squeezing the air from his lungs. He exhaled a shaky breath, unable to believe the Wakefield twins had duped him again. How could Elizabeth do this to him? It was supposed to be their special night. A night of new beginnings. She'd seemed so sincere when he'd talked to her at the beach. And he'd felt like a jerk for testing her with his stupid plan. He'd even told her he loved her, and she'd said she cared about him.

But Elizabeth must have changed her mind. His throat burned, and he closed his eyes, the romantic music and the easy laughter mocking him. He'd thought he'd been holding Elizabeth in his arms tonight, but it had been Jessica flirting with him, hanging all over him, purring in his ear. And he'd fallen right into her devious little trap. And Elizabeth had been slow dancing with Wilkins!

He slammed his punch cup down on the table, splattering red juice all over the white tablecloth and attracting a few curious stares. But he ignored the looks and stormed across the room with one simple thought spurring him on. He was going to give *Jessica* a piece of his mind.

Chapter 9

Lila was totally miserable. Forget the prom. Forget the yacht afterward. Forget Jessica Wakefield and her stupid date-stealing plans. She was going to go home, strip off this designer gown, and soak in a long bubble bath and never, *ever* think about Sweet Valley High's junior prom again. There would be other dances, other proms, other guys, other nights. . . .

Feeling close to tears, Lila hiked up the hem of her dress, ready to climb into her limo, when someone grabbed her arm. She spun around, expecting to see Jessica or one of her other friends. Instead, Courtney was standing beside her, arms crossed, her face livid. Lila gasped in surprise.

"What are you still doing here?" Lila asked.

Courtney spoke in a hushed voice. "I stayed"—she paused, glancing around—"because I'm going

127

to get revenge on Elizabeth and Todd." Her face twisted into a haughty smirk. "And I thought you might want to help."

Lila shook her head. She felt tired and weary and downright depressed. She pressed her hand to her temple, a headache pounding behind her eyes. "I just want to go home, Courtney. This prom has been a waste."

"Exactly," Courtney hissed. "That's why neither one of us *can* leave."

"Excuse me?" Lila wrinkled her forehead in confusion. "I'm not following you, Courtney. We were both dumped. We're both dressed to kill and *dateless*. And you think that's a good reason to stay?"

Courtney nodded as if her logic were totally obvious. "Yes! Todd dumped me for Elizabeth *again*, and he's not going to get away with it this time. I'm going to make him pay. And what about you, Lila?" Courtney paused to catch a breath. When she went on, her voice became more and more high-pitched. "If Jessica wasn't so selfish, you'd be here with Jordan tonight, wouldn't you?"

Lila sank back against the side of the limo, toying with the cord to her evening bag. She nodded mutely, thinking about how much she'd looked forward to this evening and how disastrously it had turned out. If it weren't for Jessica, Lila would be here with a handsome guy, dancing in his arms right now. Maybe kissing him in the moonlight.

Courtney gave a tight laugh. "Jessica is a conniving, scheming little witch. And I can't stand around and take it anymore. How about you, Lila? How many times has she left you in the lurch for her own selfish reasons? Aren't you sick of how things always work out for her?"

Lila nodded, her anger returning full force. "Yes," she mumbled. "I'd be with Jordan having a wonderful time tonight if Jessica hadn't tried to steal him from me. And he was so perfect."

"Exactly!" Courtney snapped her fingers. "Jessica always gets what she wants. Just look at her right now. We're miserable and she's with Devon, her own sister's boyfriend. You're just as beautiful and talented as she is. But she's always in the limelight when you really deserve to be."

Lila's pulse accelerated. She liked the way this girl thought.

"Well, it's the last time the Wakefield girls and Todd Wilkins make a fool out of *me*," Courtney continued. "I have a plan to make sure Jessica and Elizabeth get what they deserve."

Lila folded her arms across her chest, letting her anger invigorate her. "Just what is your plan, Courtney?"

Courtney's eyes lit up. "I'll end up with Todd, to do with as I want." Courtney leaned forward as if she was going in for the kill. "And how would you feel about ending the evening on the arm of Devon Whitelaw?"

Devon? Lila twisted her mouth in thought. *Me and Devon.* "I think I like that idea," she said. "Not only will it kill Jess, but Devon is so fine."

Courtney grinned and clapped. Lila's heartbeat picked up. She could just imagine Jessica's expression when she ended up with Devon. Her face would be as white as her dress.

"How about it, Lila?" Courtney asked, holding out her hand.

Lila clasped Courtney's hand in hers. "Just tell me what I have to do."

Elizabeth finished her sparkling cider and placed the cup near the edge of a vacant table as Todd ushered her back inside the ballroom. The dance floor was packed with couples swaying to the music. The lights had been dimmed to a level that made the stars on the wall twinkle magically.

"OK, folks, we're open to requests," the DJ interjected between songs. He spun a CD on his fingers like a top, pitched it into the air, then caught it. "Now, don't be shy. If you've got a favorite tune you want that special someone to hear, let me know." He swiveled around, and a classic Rolling Stones tune filled the room.

"At least this is one song we both agree on," Ken said with a laugh as he pulled Olivia onto the dance floor.

"Are you guys going to dance?" Elizabeth asked Enid.

Enid rolled her eyes. "I don't know. Did you see Blubber go wild earlier?"

Elizabeth laughed. "Yeah. He seems to be having fun."

Enid shrugged. "I guess so." Then she turned to Blubber. "All right, Tad," Enid said jokingly. "Let's show them how to dance. Maybe we'll start a new trend." She grabbed Blubber's hands and he followed her, looking a little awkward but excited just the same.

"I'll be right back," Todd said, dropping a kiss on Elizabeth's cheek. He disappeared into the crowd, walking toward the DJ, then came back with a grin on his face and curved his arm around Elizabeth's waist. In a few minutes the Stones song ended, and Elizabeth's heart squeezed when she recognized the song that followed. It was her and Todd's song.

"I think we should dance," Todd said quietly, looking deep into her eyes.

Elizabeth nodded, a shiver rippling up her spine at the tender way Todd was gazing at her. Laughter and soft chatter drifted around them, and Elizabeth curled into Todd's embrace and melted against him, falling into a dreamy state as their song floated through the speakers. Todd's arms tightened around her, and she lost herself in his coffee-colored eyes. His masculine cologne filled her senses, almost making her dizzy. Everything felt so right. His arms around her, their friends nearby. This was just the way she'd always imagined the junior prom would be.

Todd gently stroked her cheek, then curled the tip of her hair around his finger, and Elizabeth wet her lips in anticipation of his kiss. "You look so beautiful tonight, Liz," he said softly. His gaze was hot, lingering on her mouth, and her pulse accelerated. Then Todd angled his head and leaned down to kiss her. Elizabeth slowly closed her eyes, her heart beating furiously.

Suddenly she felt a fierce tap on her shoulder. She jerked her eyes open, almost biting her lip. Todd pulled back, his expression troubled, and she spun around to see Devon standing behind her, his eyes smoldering. "Can I talk to you for a minute, *Jessica?*"

Elizabeth's heart stopped beating and slammed into her chest. Devon knew! She could tell by the hurt darkening his expression and the angry, icy glint in his eyes.

"This isn't Jessica," Todd said, giving Devon a bewildered look.

Elizabeth froze, her stomach lurching to her throat. She opened her mouth to try to straighten things out, but Devon stopped her with a cold, furious glare.

"Really?" Devon said sarcastically. He clenched his jaw and stared hard at Todd. "Because my date said she was Elizabeth and that you were with Jessica, Todd."

"What?" Todd asked, incredulous. He gave Elizabeth a beseeching look, expecting her to deny it. "What's he talking about, Liz? You told me Devon decided he liked Jessica."

"*Me* and Jessica? I'd never date her. At least not by choice," Devon growled. Elizabeth almost withered at the disgust in his voice.

Todd shook his head, his face paling. "But it's not possible."

"Of course it's possible," Devon said sarcastically. "I'm beginning to think anything's possible with these Wakefield twins." Devon shook his head. "I should have guessed sooner. The perfume, the blatant flirting—"

"Devon, Todd, please listen. I can explain everything. . . ." Elizabeth clenched her sweaty palms together, searching for the right words to help them understand. Todd suddenly moved away from her, and she stumbled backward. She reached for him for support, but her fingertips brushed his jacket and he retreated farther, his body stiff. "Todd?"

"You don't even *like* Jessica?" Todd asked in a strangled voice, looking at Devon.

Devon let out a sound of disgust that caught several people's attention. Elizabeth winced as she realized some of the kids had stopped dancing and were staring openmouthed at the three of them. Perspiration beaded on her forehead, and she nervously tucked her hair behind her ear. She had to make them understand. "You guys . . . can we just—"

"Just what?" Todd demanded, halting her explanation with a furious glare. He glanced back at Devon. His jaw tightened. "You're saying you didn't know you were with Jessica?"

Devon shook his head. "I guess we've been duped again, man."

Todd turned to Elizabeth, and she cringed at the look of disbelief on his face. She'd never seen Todd so upset. "Why would you let Devon believe Jessica was you?"

"You don't understand," Elizabeth choked out. "I didn't want to hurt—"

"I'll tell you why," Devon snapped, his hands balling into fists. "Because sweet little Elizabeth wanted to lead us both on."

A small crowd had formed, but Elizabeth ignored them, her heart aching as she struggled to find a way out of the mess she and Jessica had created. But Todd's face suddenly lost all its color, and he turned to her again, his expression totally heartbroken. His voice sounded hoarse when he spoke. "Liz, tell me it's not true. Please, tell me . . . it's not true."

Elizabeth choked on a sob. Tears streamed down her face as she tried to think of the words to make everything right again. The mix-up over where to meet, her thinking Devon had stood her up, Todd showing up at the lake, Courtney's angry exit, Jessica going to the restaurant and pretending to be her. Everything was all a blur as her world came crashing down around her.

134

She covered her mouth, her body trembling. How could she tell Todd the truth when she didn't know what it was anymore—when she was in love with both of them, but she'd hurt them both? She looked at Devon's angry, unforgiving face, then back at Todd's devastated expression, and she realized she didn't have the words. The tension raced between them, charged and thick, filled with anger and hurt and mistrust. And it was all because of her. She suddenly felt ill. Clutching her stomach, she burst into tears, then fled out the back door.

Courtney grinned as she watched Elizabeth Wakefield get all tongue-tied, then completely fall apart right in front of Todd and everyone at the prom. Sweet Valley High would be talking about this night for a long time. It would probably make the headlines in the school paper—the very one Elizabeth worked for. And knowing she'd sparked the big blowup gave her a deep sense of satisfaction. Now for the rest of the plan.

"Wow, everything really hit the fan, didn't it?" Lila said in awe. "Devon looks like he wants to kill someone. And I've never seen Todd so upset. I bet he's going to barf."

"Yep. Devon did his part, all right," Courtney whispered gleefully. "Now it's our turn." She tugged Lila out from behind the doorway. "Just remember what I told you, Lila, and you'll get Devon. The Wakefield sisters will be all alone."

Lila nodded. "I can't wait to see Jessica's face when I steal her date and she realizes it was her *own* idea."

"One twin down, one to go," Courtney quipped, giving Lila a thumbs-up signal as she darted off.

Then Courtney eyed Todd. He was still standing in the middle of the dance floor, his shoulders slumped, his shirttail hanging loose, his tie crooked, his face ashen. He looked absolutely stricken.

A devious smile curved onto her mouth. "It serves you right for standing me up, Todd," Courtney murmured to herself. She twined her hands and waited until Devon stalked off, his cheeks flushed with anger. Then Courtney kicked up her heels and strutted across the floor, ready to set the rest of the plan into motion. Out of the corner of her eye she saw Todd drop his head and slowly leave the dance floor.

"You think you're hurting now, Todd. You haven't seen anything yet," Courtney whispered. "Just wait till *I'm* done with you."

"I'll see you guys later," Jessica said, waving to Jade Wu and some of the other cheerleaders. "I've got to get back to my date. He's probably going crazy missing me."

"See you, Jess," the girls called after her as she sauntered toward the ballroom. She was practically bouncing as she entered the room. Things between her and Devon had been going so well. Soon Devon would really be hers.

The music still wafted through the ballroom, the tunes growing softer and more romantic as the night progressed. Maybe she would request a song for her and Devon—something they could call their special song. The dance would be over soon, and they would all go to the yacht for a moonlit cruise. She couldn't wait. This night was turning out even better than she'd hoped.

But as soon as she entered the ballroom she paused. Everyone was totally quiet. An uncomfortable kind of hush filled the room that made the air feel thick and smothering. She scanned the room for Devon and spotted him talking to Winston. Devon had his head lowered and his shoulders hunched as if they were talking about something important. Probably football or motorcycles or some other boy stuff.

Since Devon had his back to her and hadn't seen her yet, she searched the room for Elizabeth. Zilch. Todd was standing in the corner with Olivia and Ken, their heads bent close. Olivia was patting Todd's back. Everyone looked so serious. Only a few couples remained on the dance floor, and most of them were simply standing there quietly, whispering and looking around. What was going on?

The music switched into an instrumental that sounded sad and melancholy, almost like funeral music. Yuck! Jessica needed to liven up this party.

"Jessica!"

Turning at the sound of her name, Jessica found Lila standing against the wall, looking nervous.

"I thought you'd left, Lila." She glared at her friend. "What do you want now?"

"I have to tell you something important," Lila snapped.

"I don't have time to talk to you now, Lila. I need to get back to Devon. I've already been gone way too long. He's probably wondering where I am."

"That's just it," Lila said in a frantic whisper that sent alarm bells ringing in Jessica's head. "Devon *is* hunting for you. But not because he's wanting to dance with you."

"What are you talking about?" Jessica asked nervously, glancing at Devon's back.

Lila gave her a sympathetic look. "Jessica, Devon *knows* about the switch."

Jessica froze, her mouth gaping open. "What? But how?" A shocking thought hit her. "It was you. You told him!"

"I did not!" Lila said indignantly.

"You did so. You were mad at me and wanted to get back at me."

Lila shook her head vigorously. "I was mad. I still *am* mad at you. But right now I'm trying to help you." She blew out a heated breath, sending a strand of hair flying away from her face. "Although I don't know why I'm doing it."

Jessica swallowed, realizing Lila was serious. "I'm sorry, Li." She bit her lip. "So . . . what happened?"

Lila folded her hands together. "Devon figured it out for himself, Jessica. Then he went over to Elizabeth and Todd and asked to speak to you—I mean, Liz."

"Oh, my gosh!" Jessica groaned.

"It was a terrible scene," Lila said. "Devon was furious. And Todd . . ."

Jessica felt sick. "Todd knows?"

"Yeah." Lila shook her head. "He wanted to know why Elizabeth let Devon think you were her, then he freaked."

"Did Elizabeth explain what happened?" Jessica asked weakly. She knew her sister couldn't talk her way out of one missed homework assignment.

"This is Liz we're talking about," Lila said. "She burst into tears and ran out of the room, sobbing."

"Oh, no!" Jessica gasped, mortified. She glanced toward the door. Her first inclination was to run for freedom herself. She didn't want to face a confrontation with Devon. He'd probably never speak to her again, and just when they were making such progress!

"I have to go," Jessica said, pulling away from Lila. "I have to get out of here and go home."

"No, you can't," Lila said in a rushed whisper. "Liz wanted you to meet her in the golf shed. She said she needed to talk to you before she ran out."

Jessica's heart melted. Poor Elizabeth. This was all her stupid idea, and now her twin had totally gone off her rocker. She was sobbing in some old garage, all alone.

"Which way did she go?" Jessica asked, deciding she'd get Elizabeth, then they'd both go home. Later, when Devon cooled off, they'd talk.

Lila pointed toward the nearest exit. "The golf shed's around that way." Lila tugged Jessica's hand. "You'd better hurry. Elizabeth was practically hysterical."

Jessica nodded just as Devon turned around and spotted her. Ken frowned, and Olivia shook her head as if she'd expected something like this from Jessica. Devon's handsome face went rigid, his cheeks flaming with anger. Jessica winced, remembering the loving way he'd been looking at her all night. Suddenly it seemed as if everyone in the room was staring at her, giving her disapproving looks. She felt as if she'd been pinned up against the wall and people were throwing darts at her from every direction.

But then she remembered Elizabeth and knew she couldn't leave her sister all alone in some stinky garage. She swallowed the bitter taste in her mouth, then raced toward the exit, ignoring her classmates—especially Devon's icy cold glare.

Chapter 10

Elizabeth covered her face with her hands, sobbing hysterically. She had retreated to the pool house and crawled into a corner on one of the benches. She'd laid her head down on her knees and let the flood of emotions welling within her loose. Now she didn't know if she would ever be able to stop. Maria and Enid hovered around her, trying to comfort her.

"Shhh, Liz, it's going to be all right," Maria said softly.

Olivia stepped in quietly and closed the door behind her.

Enid stroked Elizabeth's hair away from her face gently and handed her a tissue. "We still love you," Enid said. "And Todd and Devon will too, once they realize you didn't mean to hurt them."

Elizabeth inhaled, trying to catch her breath in

between the torrent of tears. She wadded up the Kleenex and sat, twisting it in her hands. "It's all my fault. It was so . . . so stupid," she cried. Breaking down again, she leaned against Maria, huge sobs rocking her body.

Olivia patted her back sympathetically. "You're not stupid, Liz. It was just a big mistake. When you calm down, I'm sure you'll be able to work it out."

Elizabeth shook her head, fresh tears streaming down her face. "But it's prom night . . . and I've ruined it! Because I'm such a ba-bad person." She swiped at the moisture soaking her eyes and cheeks, knowing she was probably smearing mascara all over face but not caring. What did it matter now? Bit by bit she ripped the tissue in pieces, watching morosely as the scraps fluttered to the floor. Just like her chances with Todd and Devon, the tissue was shredded and mangled.

She looked at her friends through swollen eyelids, wishing she could crawl in a hole and hide forever. "I never should have let Jessica talk me into that dumb plan of hers in the first place. Now neither one of the guys is ever going to talk to me again." She gulped, her breathing loud and erratic.

Then Lila walked in. Maria, Enid, and Olivia all turned and looked up at her expectantly.

Elizabeth opened her mouth to ask Lila about Jessica, but her words got lost on another sob. The scene in the ballroom flashed through her mind, and her heart broke all over again.

"I'm sorry about what happened," Lila said in a solemn voice. "Really, Liz."

"Oh, my gosh! Jessica!" Elizabeth started to jump up. "She doesn't know—"

Lila gently ushered Elizabeth back down to a sitting position. "Jessica knows what happened, Liz. I caught her before she went back to Devon."

"Thanks, Lila," Elizabeth mumbled.

Maria, Enid, and Olivia exchanged worried looks with Elizabeth. Elizabeth pressed her fist to her mouth to ward off another bout of crying, but a tiny sliver of hope wormed into her brain. "Is she going to talk to Devon and explain?"

Lila shook her head. "She wanted me to find you for her. She wants to talk to you—to apologize and help you figure out what to do next."

Elizabeth swallowed and wiped her eyes, then her nose. Dark mascara streaked the soaked tissue. She wadded it in her hands and stood, glancing at the pile of shredded pieces on the wooden bench. The pitiful sight made her groan. "OK, I might as well talk to Jessica. Where is she?"

"She said she'd be waiting in the golf cart garage," Lila replied, giving her another sympathetic look.

Elizabeth wrinkled her nose. The garage? That was an odd place for Jessica to go. Oh, well. Elizabeth shrugged. A dirty, smelly garage—the perfect place to be miserable. And at least it would be private.

"You'd better hurry, Elizabeth," Lila urged. "In case Devon runs into her first. Jessica seems to think if you two put your heads together, you can still fix things."

Elizabeth nodded weakly. "That sounds just like Jess. She never gives up." Maria guided her through the door. Elizabeth's head throbbed, her legs were wobbly, and she felt totally drained. "Jessica may still be plotting, but I'm going to get her and go home. I don't think there's any way to fix tonight." Elizabeth shrugged when Olivia and Enid started to protest. "It's better this way. I'm exhausted, and the whole night's a bust. Anyway, I couldn't face Todd or Devon right now."

"I'll see you later," Lila said, offering a smile as she retreated out the door.

"Come on, we'll go with you to meet Jessica," Maria said.

"Yeah, I want to make sure you find that twin of yours," Enid added sharply. "If Jessica hadn't forgotten that message, none of this would have ever happened."

Elizabeth shook her head sadly, more hot tears trickling down her cheeks. "I can't believe I lost them both. Tonight was supposed to be so special, but now it'll go down as the worst night of my life."

"Shhh. It's OK, Liz," Maria said softly. "Go home and sleep on it. You'll feel better in the morning, and so will the guys."

Enid flashed an obviously plastered-on smile.

"Let's get your sister and see if we can save her from herself."

"I'll go tell Tyler and Tad where you two are," Olivia said, rushing away.

Elizabeth nodded, too upset to speak. She just wanted to go home, crawl into bed, and stay there for the next hundred years.

"Oh, my gosh!" Lila muttered as she saw Enid and Maria leave with Elizabeth. What was she going to do now?

Lila darted back into the ballroom in a panic, her heart pounding. She had to find Courtney. They hadn't counted on Enid and Maria being with the twins. Everything could get messed up now.

Lila was in such a hurry, she bumped into Caroline—the last person she wanted to see.

"Sorry," Lila mumbled.

"How come you're in such a hurry?" Caroline asked, her natural gossip radar tuned.

"No reason," Lila said, rushing past her. "I'm just excited about the cruise."

Suzanne and Heather arched their eyebrows as she raced by, panting, but Lila ignored them and spun around, searching for her accomplice in crime. Then she spotted her—Courtney was standing near the patio, looking out at the yacht. It was already being prepared for the after-prom party! Lila dashed across the room, her heels clicking as she squeezed in between couples on the dance floor. The music was soft and slow, a romantic tune by a female vocalist that made her wish she had someone special of her own—or at least a date. Most of the couples on the floor were swaying and holding each other close. Heather Mallone and Aaron Dallas fell into each other's arms, practically making out on the dance floor.

"We have just a couple more tunes to play before we call it a night and the yacht takes off, so if you have any last minute requests, bring them up now," the DJ announced in a silky smooth voice. Lila ignored the couples and hurried toward Courtney.

"Courtney, I have to talk to you!" Lila rasped, fidgeting with the rhinestone decoration on her dress.

Courtney pivoted, her tall, curvy body silhouetted in the window light. Her smoky eyes were full of fire. "Did you do what I told you to do?" Courtney asked in a calm voice.

Lila nodded. "Yes, but there's a problem. Enid and Maria are with Elizabeth!" Lila threw up her hands in panic. "What are we going to do?"

"Settle down," Courtney responded nonchalantly. "Just go deal with Devon and Todd. I'll take care of the twins and their friends."

Lila heaved a nervous sigh, surprised at Courtney's cool control. "I hope you know what you're doing, Courtney."

Courtney gave her an airy smile, full of confidence, and lifted her head in the air. "Don't worry. Everything's under control. Now, go after Devon and keep him occupied."

Lila grinned, relaxing slightly. "I think I can do that." Then she took a deep breath and made a beeline for Devon. He was sitting slumped on a chair near the wall, his feet apart, his shoulders slouched, holding his head in his hands. She paused momentarily. He raked his hand through his hair, tousling the strands. Then his mouth turned down into a deep frown. He really looked pathetic, like he'd lost his best friend. Well, he wouldn't be sad for long. *Not with Lila to the rescue,* Lila thought.

Her job was to get Devon and Todd to go to the after-prom party on the yacht. But Devon looked so utterly miserable, how was she going to do it?

In her mind she rehearsed the plan she and Courtney had agreed on. She'd use Elizabeth. The best way to get Devon on the boat would be to tell him Elizabeth wanted his forgiveness. If she painted sweet Elizabeth as an innocent victim, the poor gullible guy would fall for it in a minute. Then, once she got him trapped at sea, she could work her womanly charms. And before the night was over, Devon would be hers!

Lila ran her fingers through her hair with a quick combing motion, then licked her lips. Satisfied that she was as irresistible as ever, she sauntered over to Devon. She was slightly disappointed that he didn't even look up when she stopped beside him, but she didn't let it dissuade her. "Devon?"

"Go away!" Devon growled without even sparing her a polite glance.

Lila squared her shoulders and forced compassion into her voice. "Listen, Devon, I'm sorry about what happened with Liz and Jessica. Switching on you was a mean thing to do, but Elizabeth is really upset."

"Well, that's too bad," Devon mumbled.

"I know you're angry, but think about it. Elizabeth is usually so sweet. She must have some kind of an explanation."

Finally Devon cut his eyes toward her. They were stony and cold. "Yeah, right."

Lila sighed dramatically. "She probably does. My guess is it has something to do with that sneaky twin sister of hers. Sometimes Liz just winds up in these messes . . . you know, because of some wild harebrained scheme of Jessica's."

Devon muttered something that Lila couldn't make out, but it didn't sound good, and she did hear Jessica's name.

She sat down in the chair beside him. "I know you feel bad now, Devon, but Liz really is hurting too. She feels terrible about what happened. She's so upset, she's been crying ever since she ran out of here. We can't get her to stop."

148

Devon raised his head and stared at her, his face hard and serious. "She *should* be crying. Who plays with people like that?" He looked down again, cradled his head in his hands, and spoke so softly, Lila had to strain to hear. "I trusted her."

"I know that," Lila said gently. "Liz truly is sorry. You should at least give her a chance to tell you what happened." She paused, scrutinizing Devon's reaction. He looked as if he might be wavering. "It's hard for her since she and Todd were together so long, but I *know* she wanted to be with you. I'm sure Jessica must have interfered somehow and messed everything up."

Devon's jaw relaxed slightly, and his eyes softened. He stared at her as if he wanted to believe her, but he was afraid to.

"Come on, go to the party," Lila coaxed, pulling at his arm. "It's prom night, and it's still early. We have the yacht waiting to take us on a cruise, and I bet you'll feel ten times better once you hear what Elizabeth has to say."

Devon shrugged. "I don't think I could feel much worse."

Lila smiled softly, covering his hand with hers. "Once you're on the boat with Liz and you talk, well, who knows? Your feelings might change."

Devon studied her for a full minute, and Lila tried not to squirm. She could see the war of emotions playing in his face. This guy really cared about Elizabeth. She felt a twinge of guilt about duping him but pushed it aside.

"All right," Devon finally agreed. "I'll go to the party and give Liz a chance to explain." He shook his head, the short strands of his hair tumbling down over his forehead, then stood. "But I'm not sure I'll ever forgive her."

Lila slipped her hand through Devon's arm. A secret smile tickled her lips as he escorted her to the door. She saw the four-hundred-foot yacht anchored at the shore and watched the waves lapping gently at the edges of the pier. A thread of excitement wove its way through her. The night had been filled with unexpected twists and turns, and so far she'd been dateless for her own party and the prom. But soon Devon would be all hers.

Jessica paced back and forth in the dingy garage, swinging her arms in frustration. She carefully dodged the clutter of tools and lawn equipment scattered around the small area so she wouldn't stain her beautiful white dress. Where was Elizabeth?

She shivered as she inspected the small space, filled with metal shelves spilling over with golf equipment, boxes of tees and balls, and gardening equipment for the golf course. She almost tripped over a Weed Wacker and shoved it out of the way with a grimace. The wretched place was dark and dirty, and there was only one lightbulb. Something gritty crunched beneath her feet, but she couldn't see what it was in the dark, and she spotted a spiderweb in the corner. Jessica paused, thinking it odd that her sister wasn't already here. After what Lila had said, she'd half expected to walk in and find Elizabeth crumpled on the floor in hysterics. The lightbulb flickered, and Jessica wrapped her arms around her middle. One more minute. She'd give Elizabeth one more—

Footsteps clicked on the concrete, jerking her from her thoughts, and she glanced up to see Elizabeth, Maria, and Enid walking through the small door. Lila had been right about one thing. Elizabeth had obviously been crying up a storm. Her eyes were swollen and red, and her makeup had taken a nosedive off her face. Her hair was mussed in all different directions, her complexion chalky white as if she'd been run through a car wash.

"Where have you been?" Jessica blurted, realizing suddenly that on top of the tense situation the cramped, dark quarters had given her the willies.

"What do you mean?" Elizabeth asked in a hoarse voice, clutching a ragged tissue in her hand. "Lila just came and told me to meet you here."

Jessica exhaled a sharp breath. "But Lila told me you were already here."

Elizabeth frowned. "I was in the pool house—"

Suddenly the door slammed behind them with a loud thud, and Jessica froze as the sound of a metal lock snapped shut. "Oh, my gosh! What's happening?" Jessica shrieked. She ran to the door and yanked on it, but it wouldn't budge.

"Jessica?" Elizabeth croaked, looking absolutely stricken. "Is it locked?"

Jessica trembled with fear, her own legs threatening to fold beneath her. Elizabeth, Enid, and Maria all gasped and turned to stare at their cramped surroundings.

"Omigosh! We're trapped!" Jessica squealed. She noticed a tiny window in the door, just big enough to peer through. Raising on her tiptoes, she peeked through the glass. Maria, Enid, and Elizabeth crowded next to her, all trying to see out the small opening at the same time.

"What is it?" Maria asked.

"What do you see?" Enid shrieked, digging her nails in Jessica's arm.

"Oww!" Jessica cried. Enid let go, and Jessica narrowed her eyes, squinting outside.

"We have to get out of here!" Elizabeth cried, kicking at the barred door with the bottom of her sandal.

Jessica peered out through the opening, straining to see. Then her eyes widened and her heart pounded so fast, she could hear it roaring in her ears. Courtney Kane was standing on the other side of the door, and the girl was waving at her!

"Courtney!" Jessica screamed. She pressed her face against the cold glass. "What are you doing?"

"Get her to unlock the door," Enid yelled.

"Help!" Maria screamed.

But Courtney simply stared at them, unmoving. "No way, girls. I hope the rest of your prom night is as magical as you dreamed," Courtney answered sarcastically.

"Courtney, I swear I'm gonna—," Jessica yelled.

"You can't do this!" Elizabeth wailed as Maria and Enid screamed. They pounded their fists and hands on the hard wood, but nothing happened. Courtney simply grinned, a snide smile that hit Jessica with renewed fear.

"Oh, a golf course worker should be by in the morning to open up," Courtney said flippantly. She tossed her hair over her shoulder and laughed. "Bye now!" She gave them a little wave, then turned away.

"No!" Jessica yelled, yanking at the door.

"Don't leave us like this," Elizabeth pleaded.

"Please, open the door," Maria and Enid cried.

"Courtney Kane, you'll be sorry!" Jessica screamed. She shivered again, thinking about how dark and dirty the little shed was. "And if I ruin my dress, I'm suing you for the cost!"

Jessica and the others kicked and pounded on the door again, beating furiously and yelling at the top of their lungs until their voices started to sound hoarse. But it was no use. Courtney had already sauntered away, her sequined dress disappearing in a brilliant flash of red like a dragon's tail disappearing into the night.

Chapter 11

Lila searched for Courtney as she and Devon left the country club and strolled onto the dock. The walk and fresh air were exhilarating, and she hated to leave Devon for even a minute, but she needed to check in with her cohort. The music died down inside and the chaperons had turned the lights back on, signifying the end of the prom. Other kids left the ballroom, and most of the couples were already walking toward the yacht.

"I'll meet you on the boat," Lila said, squeezing Devon's arm.

Devon nodded. He still looked devastated but a little more hopeful than he had earlier. He stuffed his hands in his pockets and headed down the dock.

Lila hurried away and waited next to a tall palm tree, glancing around for Courtney. Instead she saw Todd. He had his tux jacket slung over his shoulder, and he was headed toward his BMW. Oh, no. If Todd left and didn't make it to the after-prom party, Courtney would have a major fit! Plus she'd blame Lila!

Panicking, she started toward Todd, racing across the parking lot. She wove between her class-mates as they milled on the lawn and gathered in small groups on their way to the yacht. A few of her friends stopped and stared at her, but she simply waved. Her mind raced for something to say to Todd, but she couldn't think of a single way to persuade Todd to stay and go to the party. She glanced back to check on Devon and saw him hiking up the gangplank. Then she spotted Ken and Olivia. Bingo.

Lila took off to catch them, silently wishing she had some sneakers with her. When she'd strapped on her dressy heels, she imagined dancing all night, not running around chasing after people.

"The music was great," she heard Olivia say as she approached. "But kissing you is better, Ken."

Ken mumbled some nonsense and looked all goo-goo eyed. Lila wanted to gag. She grabbed his jacket sleeve, and Olivia stared at her. Ken looked irritated at having been interrupted.

"Ken, you have to do something," Lila said desperately. "Todd is leaving, and the party's not over. You have to stop him."

Ken snorted in disgust, and Olivia folded her

arms under her chest. "Well, I don't blame him," Ken muttered. "The guy's upset. And he's got a right to be after what happened."

Olivia frowned. "He probably just needs some time to settle down," she added quietly.

Lila was silently freaking. She glanced sideways and saw Todd stop at his car and dig his keys out of his pocket. Her heart raced.

"But Ken, you're Todd's best friend," Lila wailed. "You can't let him down—it's prom night." Lila grasped for a good argument. "I know Todd's upset right now, but he should be with his friends instead of all alone. He's so depressed. What if he does something stupid?"

"Todd's too smart to do something stupid, Lila. He just needs time to cool down."

But Olivia was slowly nodding in agreement with Lila. "I do hate for him to be by himself, Ken. He looks so lonely. And I don't think Liz is coming back tonight. She was a mess out in the pool house."

Ken shrugged. "Maybe he wants to be alone. He's probably had enough of girls for tonight."

"Maybe," Lila began, "but then again, he might feel better if we tried to cheer him up." She pasted on a bright smile. "After all, that's what friends are for, isn't it, Ken? Especially best friends?"

Ken stared at Lila in silence for a long minute. Lila guessed he was wondering about her motives, so she did her best to appear sincere.

"You know you and Todd go way back. You'd hate for him to write this night off like it is right now, wouldn't you?" Lila argued. "Being at the party might make him feel better instead of leaving on a sour note."

"I hate to admit it," Olivia said, "but I think Lila may have a point."

Ken grew solemn but finally nodded. "I guess you're right. Besides, I can't let him go off moping while we have fun." Ken gave Olivia a quick kiss. "I'll be right back." Then he took off jogging after Todd.

Lila held her breath while she watched Ken talk to Todd. Todd shook his head at Ken. What if Ken couldn't convince Todd to come? She chewed on her fingernail and glanced at the yacht. There were only a few more people waiting to board. They had to hurry, or they'd all miss the party.

She swung her gaze back to the guys. *Come on, Ken, come on,* she silently urged. Then Ken put his arm around Todd's shoulders, and she saw Todd shrug. She held her breath again. Finally Todd gave in and started walking toward them. Lila thought she was going to faint in relief. Finally things were going to work out!

But she glanced up and saw Olivia watching her with narrowed eyes. "Just what are you up to, Lila Fowler?" Olivia asked. "I've never seen you so concerned over someone else."

"What do you mean?" Lila asked innocently.

Olivia pierced her with a questioning stare. "It's not like you and Todd are really friends. What's up?"

"Nothing," Lila said in her most sincere voice. "But it's prom night, and we all put a lot of work into making it special. Everyone should be having fun."

And I'm just about to start having my *fun,* Lila thought.

"I can't believe this is happening," Elizabeth mumbled, sniffling. She and Maria were searching the garage for another way out while Enid and Jessica kept banging on the locked door, yelling for help.

"Help! Someone help us. We're locked inside!" Jessica screamed.

"Please get us out!" Enid wailed.

"I don't see any other door," Maria cried. She kicked at a pile of dusty cloths on the floor and sighed in despair.

"And there isn't even another window," Elizabeth added, checking the dark garage from ceiling to floor. "Just tools and a couple of stupid golf carts." She walked to the opposite side and almost tripped over an expensive leather golf bag. A putter and two other irons protruded from the bag. Two golf balls rolled out and spun across the floor, then thumped against the wall.

"Maybe we could try to drive one of those cars

159

through the garage door like they do in those action flicks," Maria suggested.

Elizabeth chuckled in spite of her increasing worry. "I think that only works in the movies. With our luck we'd tear up the carts, destroy the building, and get arrested in the process. And then we'd have to pay for damages."

"Well, at least we'd get out," Enid said drolly, wiping at a smudge of dirt darkening her cheek. "This place is not exactly the Hilton. And it's so humid, my hair is frizzing."

"It's soooo hot in here," Jessica wailed, giving Elizabeth a look of desperation. She fell against the door, sagging as if she was going to faint. "I feel like I'm smothering. I wonder how much air we have left."

Enid rolled her eyes. "Just keep yelling, Jessica, and don't get all dramatic on us. There's plenty of oxygen in here. The door even has a crack under it."

A tiny squeaking sound came from one corner. "What's that?" Jessica asked.

"Probably a mouse," Maria answered.

"Ugh!" Jessica banged on the door with renewed vigor. "Help. Please, somebody help us! There are giant rodents in here! They're going to eat us alive!"

Maria and Enid chuckled. Elizabeth checked her watch, her pulse racing as the seconds ticked by. "I can't believe it. The yacht's leaving in ten minutes. We have to get out of here *now*."

Maria slumped to a sitting position on a wooden crate, adjusting her silky dress so the fabric wouldn't snag on the loose boards. "I don't understand why Courtney did this."

"Me neither," Enid growled, leaning against a metal shelf filled with golf tees and assorted supplies. "What'd we ever do to her?"

"That girl is totally crazy," Jessica complained. "She doesn't need a reason for the things she does. She does them because she's psycho."

"I know why she did it," Elizabeth said, wincing when everyone turned to stare at her. A heavy lump settled in Elizabeth's stomach like a ball of lead. "It's because Todd ditched her. And it's my fault, *again*," she added on a shaky breath.

Elizabeth shuffled toward the window and peeked out, hope dwindling with every minute. "And right now she's out there somewhere, probably plotting revenge." She faced her sister and friends, her fears almost overwhelming her. "If Courtney gets on that boat before it takes off, there's no telling what she might do. When she gets mad, she has a terrible temper." Maria and Enid exchanged worried glances.

"You remember what happened with the rope?" Elizabeth asked.

Jessica's face paled. "You're right, Liz. She could have killed you. We have to get out!"

Elizabeth nodded, shuddering as she remembered

161

how determined Courtney had been to win the school competition. Courtney's private school, Lovett, and SVH had been competing in an interschool obstacle race. The gym had been set up with an elaborate course, and when it had been Elizabeth's turn to climb the rope, she'd gotten halfway to the top and the rope had frayed and broken. She'd fallen several yards to the floor.

She still remembered the paralyzing fear she'd felt just before she'd hit the floor. Todd had come running to her rescue, upset and worried about her, making Courtney even more furious. Then they'd discovered that Courtney had substituted an old, worn rope in place of the new one that Elizabeth was supposed to climb. So her accident hadn't been an accident but a deliberate attempt on Courtney's part to hurt her and score points for her team. What else was Courtney capable of?

Jessica started banging on the door again, yelling at the top of her lungs.

"Maybe Devon will come looking for you," Maria suggested.

Elizabeth looked at her hands sadly. "I doubt it," she mumbled, feeling tears sting her eyes again. "He was so upset and hurt. Even if he doesn't want to go out with me again, I have to find him and explain so he doesn't think I hurt him on purpose."

Maria patted her shoulder. "Don't worry, Liz. We'll find him when we get out."

"Somehow it's going to work out," Enid said encouragingly.

Suddenly Jessica shrieked and jumped up and down. "Wait, you guys. I see someone coming!"

Enid and Maria and Elizabeth ran to the little window, hovering near the glass, all trying to look over Jessica's head.

"It's Blubber and Tyler!" Maria screamed.

"I knew they'd come looking for us," Enid exclaimed. "I've never been so glad to see Blubber in my life."

The girls frantically pounded on the door and screamed all at once.

Tyler and Blubber ran up to the door. Jessica stuck her face in the window and motioned toward Elizabeth, Enid, and Maria. The three girls waved frantically, all pointing to the locked doorknob. The door rattled as Tyler and Blubber struggled to open it, but the knob wouldn't turn.

"Open it!" Jessica yelled.

"Hurry!" Elizabeth screamed, wedging her face into the window beside her twin's. "We have to get to the yacht."

"It's locked. I'll go for help," Tyler called. He gave Maria a warm, tender smile. "Don't worry, Maria; I'll get you out."

Enid grinned, and Elizabeth squeezed Maria's arm. "He really likes you."

Maria blushed. "He's pretty cool. But right now I'd settle for him getting us out of here."

"Stand back!" Blubber ordered, his cheeks ballooning out in determination. He took off his coat and laid it on a nearby chair. "I'm going to try to break down the door!"

The girls nodded, clutching each other as they backed away and stared at the unbending heavy wood. Jessica grabbed Elizabeth's arms, her fingernails biting into Elizabeth's wrist. A loud slam reverberated through the tiny room as Blubber hurled his two-hundred-plus pounds against the door frame. Elizabeth tensed, noticing Enid and Maria suck in loud breaths. They were probably expecting to hear the wood crackle and splinter at any second, just like she was. Elizabeth pictured Blubber crashing through the door and the four of them rushing toward him as he sprawled onto the floor in victory.

But nothing happened. The thick structure barely flexed under his weight. Jessica shrieked; Enid and Maria gasped. Elizabeth exhaled sharply, clenching her hands together as if she could send him extra strength just by wishing it. Elizabeth and Enid ran to the window, and Elizabeth was relieved to see that Blubber was OK. Then Blubber stepped back with obvious determination, and the girls moved out of the way again.

"Come on, you can do it, Tad," Enid whispered.

"Hit it hard!" Jessica yelled.

"Hurry!" Maria screamed.

The force of his weight hit the wood with a

sickening thud. Still nothing, but Blubber kept trying.

"Come on," Enid rasped.

Elizabeth squeezed her eyes shut, remembering the angry glint in Courtney's smoky eyes as
she'd walked away from the locked door. *Please
hurry*, Elizabeth urged Tad silently. *Courtney's
dangerous. There's no telling what else she has
planned for tonight.*

Devon kept his eyes trained on the gangplank,
watching each person who walked on the dock,
expecting to see Elizabeth at any minute. But so
far half the cheerleaders, most of the football
team, Winston, Maria, and a herd of other Sweet
Valley students had crossed the dock and entered
the yacht. What was keeping Elizabeth? Lila had
said she was upset, but he'd thought she'd be
here by now.

Suddenly he caught sight of a long black dress
and saw Lila's dark hair catch in the light flickering
off one of the deck lamps. She scurried up the
gangplank with a grin on her face and walked
straight toward him, her hips swaying under the
tight fabric of her dress. How in the world did she
breathe in that thing?

"Where's Liz?" he asked before Lila even had a
chance to speak.

Lila gave him one of her serene smiles. "Oh,
she'll be along." She glanced around the outer

deck as if she was searching for Elizabeth. "That is, if she's not here already. Maybe you missed her coming onboard."

"I don't think so." Devon tilted his head and scanned the boat, his eyes filtering through the crowd for Elizabeth's shimmering lavender dress. But he didn't see Elizabeth or her evil twin. "Maybe you're right," he mumbled. "There's a lot of people here. I think I'll go look for her."

"No," Lila protested, gently slipping her hand into the crook of his arm. "Wait here with me for a while. At least until the rest of my friends show. I really hate to stand here all alone."

Devon shrugged. He had no desire to stay there with Lila, who he figured was just as devious as Jessica and twice as spoiled. But then again, Elizabeth had been the one to trick him. He shouldn't go running after her. It was up to *her* to come looking for *him*.

"So, how do you like SVH?" Lila asked.

Devon arched an eyebrow, curious at her sudden interest. He hated small talk. "It's OK. My classes are pretty cool. It's better than Westwood Academy."

He noticed Todd, Ken, and Olivia climb onto the gangplank and head toward the rear deck. Todd still looked dejected. But as much as Devon felt sorry for the guy, a little seed of hope sprouted inside. Elizabeth wasn't with Todd anymore. Maybe she *was* coming to see him. Maybe it had been a horrible misunderstanding like that night at the beach.

But his old cynical voice wormed inside his head, taunting him. *And maybe she's playing you for a sucker.*

"My father wanted me to go to one of those private schools," Lila said. She smiled demurely, flipping a strand of her dark hair over one bare shoulder and posing almost dramatically, like one of those fashion models in a magazine. "But I thought it would be better to experience real high-school life."

"Really?" Devon asked, barely hiding the sarcasm in his voice. "It's very noble of you to want to mingle with the commoners." She didn't even seem to register his dig.

"Yes, well, SVH is a great school." She batted her lashes at him, and Devon's hand tightened around the rail. "Of course, my father makes regular donations to the board of education."

Devon couldn't believe Lila was flirting with him—trying to impress him with her father's wealth. He bit off the urge to tell her how very unimpressed he was.

"You know my dad has his own yacht. And he and my mom travel constantly. They have a hundred-and-thirty-foot Viking docked off the coast of Singapore. I'm probably the most worldly girl at SVH," she continued.

Devon swallowed the distaste burning his throat and strove to maintain his manners. "Yeah?"

Lila ran a manicured fingernail over his knuckles and positioned herself seductively against him, her leg brushing up against his thigh. Devon's stomach churned. What was with these girls? Didn't they have any respect for their friends' feelings?

Lila kept chattering, some nonsensical drivel that he could care less about, even speaking a few words of French, trying to impress him. He muttered a response in the same language, which obviously fueled her for another few minutes. Then out of the corner of his eye he caught a glimpse of something flashy and bright red. Courtney Kane was sashaying onto the boat, her very short, extremely tight dress hugging her hips as she walked. Devon frowned, wondering what she was still doing here. She didn't even go to SVH. Yet she glided up the breezeway as if she owned the world and the rest of the students onboard were awaiting her arrival.

Devon started to look away, but then he realized Courtney was staring right at him, and the icy glint in her eyes made his blood run cold.

Lila cuddled even closer to him as Courtney walked by. Devon could've sworn he saw Courtney wink at Lila. What were these girls up to?

Chapter 12

"I can't believe you can maul those two-hundred-pound guys on the football team and you can't break down a measly door!" Jessica yelled at Blubber. Her heart was beating furiously, and she twisted her sweaty hands together, stifling a wave of tears. The night was a disaster, she was getting dust on her beautiful white dress, and the dank air in the garage was suffocating her. If he didn't get the door open soon, she was going to totally freak.

"He's trying," Elizabeth told Jessica, patting her on the back. But Elizabeth's voice was shaky, and Jessica knew her sister was about to lose her cool too.

Maria rose on tiptoes, searching through the window. "Tyler will come through, I just know it."

"He'd better," Jessica mumbled.

"Come on, Tad," Enid urged. "You can do it!"

Elizabeth and Maria held their breath as Blubber hit the door and bounced off it one more time.

"Use your weight!" Jessica screamed.

"He is!" Enid bellowed at Jessica.

"Let's not yell at each other," Elizabeth pleaded.

Just then Tyler came running back with a man dressed in army green work clothes, dangling an enormous gold ring that held what appeared to be a hundred different keys.

"It's the groundskeeper!" Elizabeth shouted.

"Hurry up," Jessica urged as she saw the short, gray-haired man fumble with the ring of keys, searching for the right one. He tried a square key, but it didn't work, then held the gold chain up and jangled them, peering at the massive collection as if he didn't have a clue.

Jessica sighed in frustration. They had to hurry! Courtney and Lila had already gotten on that boat, and if she was going to kill them, which she *was* definitely going to do as soon as she found them, she had to get on that boat too! She squeezed her fist around the doorknob as she heard the keys rattle again while the groundskeeper inserted another one into the lock, working to open it. The nerve of Courtney. Locking her and Elizabeth into a stinky garage on prom night. And Lila! Some best friend!

Elizabeth was right. Courtney was probably

sinking her hooks back into Todd, taking advantage of the poor hapless sap just when he was down. They had to get to the boat before it left. Even boring-as-butter Todd didn't deserve the likes of Courtney Kane—monster man-eater! The poor guy would probably be so sidetracked by her skimpy red dress that he wouldn't recognize the kind of vindictive mind he was up against until it was already too late.

"Come on, come on, come on," Elizabeth, Enid, and Maria whispered all at once.

Jessica stared at the keyhole with all her might, as if she could will it to open. The sound of metal clinking on the other side made her suck in her breath. Finally she heard a click and saw the knob being twisted. The door swung open. Jessica sprang outside, gasping for air. The others rushed out behind her.

Tyler hugged Maria, and Enid threw her arms around Blubber. "Thank you, Tad. You were great."

"Come on!" Elizabeth yelled, grabbing Enid by the wrist. "We don't have time to stand and talk. We have to stop Courtney!"

Jessica, Elizabeth, Enid, Maria, Tyler, and Blubber went tearing off across the lawn, heading for the dock.

"Oh, my gosh! They're pulling up the plank!" Jessica shouted as the dock came into view. "Stop! You can't leave us!"

"Don't go!" Elizabeth shouted. The others

yelled at the boat too, all of them waving their arms frantically to get someone's attention.

"Hey, hold up!"

"Look at us!"

"Wait!" Jessica yelled again, sprinting onto the dock. She gauged the distance and realized they still had to run all the way to the end. Her stomach jumped into her throat at the sound of the ship's horn signaling its departure. It was hopeless!

Still, she hiked up her dress and sprinted forward, shouting and waving. The others' heels pounded on the wooden dock behind her as they tore down the plank at full speed. Maria and Enid shouted and waved, their dresses flapping in the wind. But their cries lost momentum as they were caught in the breeze coming off the ocean, and Jessica realized the sound was probably being swept away.

She froze and came to a stop, throwing her hands above her head and jumping up and down to signal the boat. The others rushed up beside her and joined in.

"No," Elizabeth whispered, wheezing as she halted beside Jessica. "No, you can't leave."

Jessica leaned over the edge and peered at the rim of the yacht as it glided farther out to sea. Squinting, she glanced across the crowded deck and spotted two people standing off to themselves. Lila's striking dark hair and black dress were illuminated by a sliver of moonlight. Jessica froze as she recognized the guy beside Lila. It was Devon!

Lila and Devon were standing so close, with their heads bent together, almost touching. Jessica's chest heaved. She had never been more livid in her entire life. She whirled around and saw Elizabeth's pale face turn ghostly white and knew Elizabeth had seen Devon and Lila together too.

What were they going to do now?

Courtney fluttered her long lashes and pasted on a beguiling smile, unable to believe what a total sap Todd was. All she had to do was tell him she could help him forget Elizabeth. That and one look at her sexy dress, and he was following her around like a whipped puppy dog.

"We're going down to the lower level," Olivia said, clasping Ken's hand in hers and shooting Courtney a curious glance.

Ken winked. "See you later, man."

Todd nodded. "I'm glad you talked me into coming."

"I bet you are," Ken said with a laugh. He gave Courtney a once-over appraisal, then flicked Todd a thumbs-up signal.

Todd wrapped his arm around Courtney's waist.

"See you guys later," Courtney said with a wave.

"I sure am glad you decided to come onboard," Todd said, leaning closer to Courtney as the yacht changed course slightly. "I'm already starting to feel better. I hope you'll forgive me for what I did earlier."

Courtney drew a small circle on Todd's chest with her finger. "Todd, I'm glad you're feeling better. And I wouldn't miss this cruise for the world."

"How could a guy feel depressed when he has someone as gorgeous as you standing beside him?" Todd asked with a teasing grin.

Courtney smiled, tracing a path down his dark jacket sleeve with her finger. "So now we can finally be together."

"Yep. I'm finished with Elizabeth Wakefield for good. I can't believe I actually felt sorry for her earlier. That's the reason I decided to take her to the prom, Courtney." Todd brushed a strand of her hair over her shoulder, his dark brown eyes raking over her, then settling at the low neckline to her skintight dress.

"When Liz got all upset, I thought I was being a nice guy. But she was just using me, playing with my feelings. Good old dependable Todd." His mouth tightened into a frown. "But that's over. And seeing the two of us back together should really get to her. I'll show her she can't use me whenever she needs a fill-in."

Courtney's already hardened heart squeezed tighter. *A fill-in.* Just the way he'd used her! Only now he'd been burned by Elizabeth and he was falling for her, hook, line, and sinker.

A salty breeze from the ocean sprayed the deck

as they hit a big wave, and Todd pulled her close to him, shielding her from the moisture. Todd was trying to act tough, like he was just hanging out with her to get back at Elizabeth, but she could tell he thought she was sexy. Of course, she'd counted on that when she bought the dress. If Elizabeth Wakefield hadn't interfered, Todd would never have been able to resist Courtney all night.

She glanced around and noticed some of the couples heading inside to the main cabin, others filing down the steps to the lower deck. "Let's check this baby out," Todd said, patting the fiberglass siding.

Courtney nodded, and they toured the three-story yacht. The entire ship was designed for entertaining. The top floor housed a heated pool, Jacuzzi, and comfortable lounging area; the middle floor boasted a luxurious dining room, bar, and snack tables. It was decorated in teak woods and contemporary paneling with soft, inviting colors. Also several smaller lounging berths were open, equipped with game tables, TVs, and cozy seating areas.

The lower deck was designed for strolling and water-accessible sports. As they toured the boat Courtney noticed kids clustered in groups on the deck and in the lounges. There were even a few guys planted in front of the large-screen TV in the main lounge.

Todd threaded his fingers through hers, and

Courtney gave him her most demure smile as she tugged gently on his hand. "Let's go someplace a little more private," she whispered huskily.

A spark of excitement lit Todd's eyes, and he winked. "Lead the way, Courtney. I'm tired of the crowd."

Courtney made sure her hips swayed in just the right enticing way as Todd followed her down the winding staircase to a deck where a few love-birds were already snatching some privacy. Ken and Olivia were nestled in each other's arms on a long vinyl sofa. Two cheerleaders she recognized were snuggled with their boyfriends. And that weird guy, Winston, and his date were strolling along the deck, hand in hand, oblivious to anyone else. The atmosphere was perfect.

She inched farther down the deck to a shad-owed corner not visible from the open lounge. Catching sight of a slim wooden railing, she hoisted herself up, tilting her head back seduc-tively as the evening breeze whipped her hair around her face. She imagined herself posing for a fashion magazine and stretched out her long legs, arching her back. She saw Todd hitch in a breath and color flame his adorable cheeks. She also saw his eyes widen in alarm when she teetered slightly. He relaxed as she caught the rail to steady herself, and she let herself enjoy the power she had over him.

"Um, Courtney, maybe you'd better come

down from there," Todd said in a rush.

Courtney laughed softly. She'd known Todd would be beguiled by her, but she also knew her behavior would make him nervous. He was so *predictable!*

"Oh, but Todd, it feels so wonderful up here." She threw her hands up in a mock gesture of wild abandon. "I feel like I'm being swept away by the ocean, free and incredibly alive."

Todd swallowed nervously.

"You should come up here, Todd. It's amazing." Curling one hand around the rail for balance, she reached for Todd with the other. "Come on, Todd, you aren't with boring Elizabeth Wakefield anymore. You're with Courtney Kane, and we're going to live it up!"

Todd hesitated, but her last words were just the challenge needed to persuade him. Todd nodded, a look of determination spreading on his face. "You're right. Tonight's the night for fun, and I can't think of anyone more exciting than you."

Todd gripped the slim wooden railing with both hands, turned sideways, and hoisted himself up. He was bigger than Courtney, and he had a hard time settling his weight evenly, but he finally balanced himself and scooted closer to her.

"You're right, Courtney. It's great," Todd said, jutting his hand up to feel the soft breeze. He wobbled but quickly grabbed the rail, clutching it tightly.

You're steady now, Todd, Courtney thought, giving him an encouraging smile. *But not for long.*

Elizabeth watched the magnificent yacht drift farther and farther out to sea, and a surge of pure panic clawed at her insides. They weren't going to make it. She momentarily sagged against a lamppost, feeling weary and defeated, but she remembered the evil gleam in Courtney's eyes and told herself not to give up. She had to catch that boat and find out what Courtney was up to.

"Liz, what are we doing to do?" Jessica shrieked, throwing her hands up in the air.

Enid, Maria, and their dates were still yelling and waving frantically, trying to draw someone's attention. Quickly Elizabeth scanned the dock and surrounding area. Two sailboats registered in her vision, but sailboats wouldn't do them any good. The yacht would be miles out to sea before they even had the sails raised. She glanced a few feet beyond and spotted a rental area. Bikes, Jet Skis, speedboats. *Speedboats!*

"Come on! I have an idea," Elizabeth said, motioning for the others to follow her as she raced toward the rental booth.

"Wait for me!" Jessica cried. But Elizabeth was already halfway down the dock. She opened her purse, pulled out every dime of her spending money for the weekend, and slapped it into the palm of the guy working the rental booth.

The short, stout man scratched his cap of dark hair and arched an eyebrow. "Ma'am, we're about to close for the night. Can you come back tomorrow?"

"No, I can't!" Elizabeth's heart pounded. "You have to let us take a boat! It's an emergency!"

Jessica and the others barreled up behind her. "We need to hurry!" Jessica shouted.

"Liz, I think I'm losing sight of them!" Maria cried.

"Mister, we need that boat," Blubber said in his deep voice.

The man drew back at Tad's size, then seemed to take stock of their panicked faces, wadded the money in his hand, and handed Elizabeth a set of keys. "You do know how to drive one of these?"

"Of course." Elizabeth hiked up her dress, then scampered across the dock and hopped in the first boat.

"Thank you, sir," Tyler said, shaking the man's hand heartily.

"You be careful," the man warned sternly.

Blubber jumped into the boat and sent it rocking with his bulk. But he quickly steadied it, held out his arms, and helped Jessica, then Enid and Maria onboard. Maria nearly stumbled, but Tyler caught her, scooped her in his arms, and swung her onto one of the benched seats, then climbed over beside her.

"Hurry, Liz!" Jessica screamed.

"Everyone put their life preservers on!" Elizabeth ordered. A gust of wind tossed her hair around her face, and she shoved the strands behind her ears, ignoring the salty sting of the water as it sprayed into her eyes. "Hold on, I'm putting it in high speed."

"Do you want me to drive?" Tyler shouted.

Elizabeth shook her head, jamming the key into the ignition. When the motor roared to life, she slammed the gearshift into full throttle and took off through the surf. The boat jerked as she increased the speed and rocked over the waves. "No, but you'd better sit down!" She squinted through the darkness, zeroing in on the tail end of the yacht. It wasn't that far away. There was still a chance.

Her stomach clenched into a tight knot and she ground her teeth together as different scenarios raced through her mind. What if Courtney totally lost it like she had with the rope incident? Or worse?

"Come on, Liz!" Jessica urged.

"She's doing the best she can," Tyler shouted.

Elizabeth glanced over her shoulder and saw Enid cuddled in Tad's large arms as he tried to shield her from the salt and water pelting their clothes and hair. Maria hovered near Tyler, her eyes wide and alert. Jessica was shivering violently, her hair and clothes already damp from the dewy ocean spray, her cheeks unnaturally pale.

A rush of water sprayed the front of the boat as they flew through the surf, and Elizabeth winced as it hit her bare arms and drenched the skirt of her gown. But she stayed focused, concentrating on steering the boat through the rolling waves and guiding them safely toward the yacht. She would worry about everyone's hair and clothes later. Right now she had to make sure Courtney hadn't pulled anything equally messed up on Todd!

Tiny lights flickered from the yacht's stern, and she veered the speedboat a few degrees to the left so she wouldn't get caught in the tailwind. She was getting closer, so close she could now make out the red lettering on the side of the boat. They hit a wave and the boat rocked, pitching everyone forward. She heard screams behind her, and the water once again splashed aboard and drenched her dress and face, but she clenched her hands so tight her knuckles whitened and jerked the steering wheel to the right, hanging on as the boat tipped sideways. When the boat leveled out, she licked the salty water from her lips and sighed in relief. "Everybody OK?" Elizabeth shouted over her shoulder.

"We're fine!" Maria shouted.

Elizabeth's arms ached from trying to hold the boat steady against the raging water, but the hum of the motor gave her comfort, and when she finally spotted the outline of people onboard the deck, she downshifted.

"We're almost there!" she yelled.

"Be careful," Tyler shouted.

"Get closer," Jessica pleaded.

As they came up alongside the boat, Elizabeth glanced up and saw people milling around the middle deck. The yacht seemed enormous. Todd and Courtney could be anywhere.

Then she spotted a couple on the lower deck. Olivia and Ken, maybe? For a moment she thought she heard the faint sound of music, but the wind drowned out the tune, and she wondered if she'd imagined it.

"Get closer!" Jessica shouted again.

"I'm trying!" Elizabeth yelled. She winged the boat to the right again, setting it within a few hundred feet of the side of the yacht. The speedboat suddenly seemed dwarfed by the massive yacht, and she slipped the boat into low gear, then killed the engine so they could drift closer to the edge. She hurriedly glanced up to check out the deck again. Leaning back, she spotted couples strolling on the upper level; others lingered in corners and on outside benches, hugging and talking and making out.

Then Elizabeth gasped as she saw something she couldn't believe. Todd and Courtney were perched on the railing in a deserted area near the rear of the boat. As Elizabeth watched, horrified, Todd leaned in for a kiss. The last thing she'd expected to find was a romantic moment—she'd been worried that Todd could be in danger! A streak of jealousy slammed into her. But before she could even register the hurt, Elizabeth's eyes were met by a far more terrifying sight. In a flash Todd's body had tumbled off the railing and was plummeting down at an incredible speed! He screamed and flailed his arms as he plunged into the ocean. A loud splash sent a shower of water against the side of the yacht. Almost immediately Todd disappeared into the sea. His screams died as he was dragged under the rolling waves.

"Todd!" Elizabeth shouted. Through a haze of fear she could hear everyone around her yelling and her twin's voice shrieking, "He's going to drown!"

Elizabeth didn't stop to think. She dove over the side of the boat to go after him, grateful that she still had her life jacket on. But just as she plunged into the icy water, she thought she saw Courtney look over the edge—and smile.

Chapter 13

Devon was getting nervous. Elizabeth had never showed, and Courtney had looked far too self-satisfied for his liking. Lila's flirting was becoming intolerably annoying, and he'd begun to wonder if she had told him the truth. Did Elizabeth really want to explain things to him? And if she had, then where was she?

His first thought was that Elizabeth might have gone to see Todd, but he'd seen Wilkins with Courtney earlier. Still, maybe Todd knew what had happened to Elizabeth. Or maybe Courtney knew, although Devon almost hoped that wasn't the case.

Lila said something in a dramatic tone about seeing a fashion show in Paris, and Devon made a decision.

"I'm going to look for Todd," he said abruptly. He turned to leave, but Lila followed on his heels.

"I'll . . . uh . . . I'll come with you," she stammered.

Devon's skin crawled. There was definitely something wrong here. He could feel it. He walked all over the upper level, but he didn't see Todd anywhere. In one of the enclosed staterooms he noticed a bunch of guys talking over football plays. That gossip queen, Caroline, was cuddled with her date on a comfortable-looking love seat, but he didn't see Enid or Maria or their dates. That was odd. And no Elizabeth.

An uneasy feeling settled in his stomach.

"Maybe they went below," Lila suggested, dogging him as he swung around and started the other way.

He nodded, then poked his head into the cabin upstairs. A few couples were sitting around talking, listening to CDs on the stereo and eating at the snack bar. Penny and her date were slow dancing, and Winston and Maria were cuddled on the sofa, feeding each other pretzels.

"Let's go downstairs and look for them." The nervous feeling in Devon's stomach ballooned as he headed down the circular staircase. Lila's shoes clicked on the metal steps behind him. He looked up one side of the deck, then down the other, weaving past a few couples who had decided to find a little privacy in the moonlight—something he'd planned to be doing with Elizabeth before the whole night had been shattered.

"Devon," Lila whined, pulling on his sleeve. "I don't see them anywhere. Let's find a place to sit and talk, just the two of us."

"I have to see if Elizabeth's here. And where could Todd have gone?" He stopped so suddenly, Lila bumped into him. A spark of red flashed in the moonlight. It was Courtney. She sat on the railing with her dress hiked halfway up her rear, grinning crazily. And he thought he saw someone else in the shadows, but then a movement caught his eye—it looked like a shoving motion. Courtney slapped her hands together in satisfaction, and behind him a scream pierced the air. He pivoted to see Lila shouting, a panic-stricken look on her face.

"No, Courtney!" Lila screamed again.

Devon raced forward, glancing over the edge of the railing. He thought he saw something hit and splash into the water. A body. Todd! Devon grabbed Courtney's arm and jerked her off the railing. "What did you do? That was Todd, wasn't it? He was sitting with you!"

Courtney merely smiled at him. Her eyes looked wild and glazed, and she let out a hideous, evil laugh that knotted his stomach. "Courtney, was that Todd?" Devon shouted, tightening his grip on her arms. "Did you push him overboard?"

"Someone went overboard!" a voice shouted.

"Who was it?" another voice shrieked. Chaos quickly descended, and the once deserted deck was flooded with students screaming and asking questions. "What's going on?"

"What happened?"

"Who screamed?"

"Are you OK, Lila?"

Their classmates gathered around, all trying to find out what had happened, but Lila stood paralyzed, the color draining from her face. Then she burst into tears.

"Todd went over the side!" Devon yelled. "Somebody get help! Hurry!"

A few guys sprang into action, running in different directions to find help.

Winston and Maria raced up to Devon. "Are you sure it was Todd?" Maria asked, horrified. Devon nodded, and Maria huddled against Winston.

Winston leaned over the side, searching the water. "Jeez, man, where is he?"

A crew member suddenly appeared, his eyebrows wrinkled in concern. "You sure someone went over, young man?"

Devon nodded, glaring at Courtney. "Yes. A guy named Todd Wilkins."

The man pulled a flashlight from his belt and switched it on. "Where did he fall from?"

"Right there." Devon pointed to the space where Courtney had been sitting. Then sirens fired up and blared loudly while people shouted orders behind him. Courtney tried to squirm away from

Devon, but he jerked her still and tightened his hold. "You're not going anywhere, Courtney. Not until you admit what you did."

"But I didn't do anything," Courtney protested. "You're crazy! Let me go!" She wiggled again, pummeling Devon with her fists, but Devon dug his fingers into her arms, determined to make her admit her actions. Out of the corner of his eye he saw a member of the crew dive into the water at the spot he'd indicated.

Lila stepped forward, her shocked expression frightening him even more. She sniffed, then spoke in a wobbly voice. "Courtney, I didn't know you were going to try to *kill* him."

"Shut up!" Courtney bellowed. "I didn't do anything!"

Lila's dark eyes widened in alarm, and she broke down and sobbed again, pressing her hand over her mouth.

"You knew she planned this?" Devon asked Lila, a lump of fear growing in his throat.

"Lila, how could you?" Maria Santelli asked.

Lila shook her head adamantly. "No, I knew she was upset. That she was planning *something* all night, but I didn't know what. I never guessed she'd do something like this. . . ." Her last words broke on another sob.

Two more crew members rushed up, while below, the crew lowered a life raft. "Can you tell us what happened?" the men asked.

Devon pulled Courtney forward. "This girl pushed a guy over the edge, that's what happened. She tried to kill him."

"I did not!" Courtney argued, flailing her arms at him. "He's crazy! Some kind of lunatic!"

"The guy's name is Todd Wilkins," Devon said calmly, staring at Lila for support.

"He's right," Lila said, pointing to Courtney. "She pushed him. Please, you have to rescue him," Lila pleaded.

"Miss, you're going to have to come with us," one of the men ordered, taking Courtney's arm.

"No, I won't!" Courtney screamed, and tried to wrench herself away.

But the men hauled her off, kicking and screaming and protesting the whole time.

Lila's terrified sobs escalated. Devon put his arm around her. "Shhh, Lila, they'll find Todd," he said softly. "There's a whole crew working to rescue him."

"But . . . it's not just Todd," Lila cried. "It's . . . I can't believe this is happening."

"What are you talking about?" Devon asked, his heart once again pounding out of control.

"Jessica . . . and Liz," Lila blurted between hiccupy sobs. "They're locked up. . . ."

"They're what?" Devon asked, his voice escalating with panic.

Lila sniffled, her breath bursting out in short waves as more tears flowed. "With Enid and

Maria . . . locked up . . . back at the country club."

Devon tensed and curled his hands around Lila's arms, struggling to keep his fears in check. Elizabeth's warning about Courtney reverberated in his head. *"Courtney is dangerous."* What if Courtney had hurt Elizabeth? Or worse? What would he do without her? He cleared his throat, barely able to speak. "Liz is locked up at the country club? Where, Lila?"

Lila continued to sob. "I'm sorry . . . so sorry. . . . I didn't know Courtney—"

"Forget Courtney, Lila!" he yelled, tempted to shake her. "Just tell me where Liz and the others are! Are they hurt?"

"No. They're locked in the garage . . . at the country club," Lila sobbed.

"I don't believe you people!" Devon said through clenched teeth. He wanted to scream and rant and hit something, but he realized quickly that somebody had to get back and let the girls out. He released Lila and flagged down one of the crew members who was supervising the rescue attempt. "Do you have a speedboat onboard?"

The man arched a brow at him and nodded. "Yes, sir, but it's only for emergencies."

"This is an emergency!" Devon shouted, his pulse thumping crazily. After what Courtney had just done to Todd, who knew what she had planned for Elizabeth? "Some other kids could be in danger back onshore."

The man nodded curtly, then motioned for him to follow. "I'll take you to the shore."

"I'm coming too," Lila said, clasping his arm.

Devon sighed in frustration, then looked at how petrified Lila was. This wasn't the time to be angry with her. He slipped an arm around her shoulders again, trying to stop her tears as the crewman led them to where the speedboat was stowed. He exhaled a sharp breath when he saw the crew open the hatch. Lila leaned against him, trembling all over.

Devon watched the crew release the speedboat from the storage area into the water beside the yacht. He descended the rail leading into the boat after the crewman was onboard, then helped Lila in beside him. "Put a life jacket on," he ordered Lila. With one swift motion the crewman started the engine, and the boat hurled away from the yacht.

He had to find Elizabeth and the others and get them out. He just hoped they were OK. Maybe once he found them, they could all talk this whole thing out and put this weird night behind them.

Elizabeth paddled fiercely against the waves, pumping her legs and arms, desperately trying to reach Todd. "Todd! Todd! I'm right here!" A wave rolled over her and she coughed, spitting out the salty water, almost losing her breath as she saw Todd dragged underneath a wave.

She swam harder, kicking and struggling, determined to reach him before he was lost in the current. Waves raged around her, the sound almost deafening as she shouted for Todd. Could he even hear her? Did he know she was trying to save him?

Finally she managed to swim close enough to Todd. He was struggling to stay afloat and quickly losing the battle. She snagged a piece of his jacket and curled her fingers in it, holding on to it with every ounce of strength she possessed. The current was so strong it caught her and pulled her under, but she held her breath, fighting again so she wouldn't lose her grip on Todd. The waves crashed and rolled around her, and she almost lost him several times, but she prayed fiercely and managed to hold on. Resurfacing after a big wave, she coughed and gasped for air, clamping onto Todd's arm with her hand. He moaned, trying to swim, but his body was limp, and she knew he couldn't fight the strong current. She was having enough trouble, and she had a life jacket on.

"Hang on, Todd, we're almost there!" Elizabeth yelled over the wind as she spotted a rescue boat being lowered beside the yacht.

"Come on, Liz, you can make it," Maria shouted from the boat. Elizabeth glanced up through the haze of water and saw that the rest of her friends were in the rescue boat. Relief and renewed determination filled her. Only a few more yards. She could make it. She had to. She couldn't let Todd down—not this time.

Todd moaned again and she continued to swim, battling the raging waves, ignoring the biting cold as she dragged him to safety. Her muscles ached, but she spotted two crewmen from the ship leaning over to help them in and knew it was worth it. One of them reached for Todd, and she pulled Todd in front of her, then shoved him from behind. He flailed his arms in an attempt to crawl up, but he was so weak, his hands slipped off the boat. His body felt heavy and weighted, and she was afraid he might have already swallowed too much water. The crewman grabbed his arm and kept him from sinking.

"I've got him!" the man yelled. One man tugged on Todd's arms while the second leaned over the edge of the boat, reached down and nabbed the back of Todd's coat, and hauled him inside to safety. Maria, Enid, Tad, and Tyler cheered, then quickly gathered around him.

"He's OK!" Enid shouted.

"You did it, Liz," Enid yelled.

Elizabeth shoved several soggy strands of hair from her face and swam toward the edge of the boat, her movements made slow and awkward by the cumbersome life preserver. The crew members were checking Todd and already were wiping his face with a towel and patting him down, trying to warm him. She clung to the side of the rescue boat, staring at his face, making sure he was alive.

"Liz?"

When Elizabeth heard Todd's raspy voice call her name, her heart swelled. "I'm here, Todd. You're going to be OK now." Elizabeth blinked at the tears forming in her eyes while she treaded water.

"Thanks . . ." Todd coughed, spitting out water. He glanced over at her, and Elizabeth smiled. She'd been so scared when she'd seen Todd go over, so afraid she wouldn't reach him in time. But she had. She'd saved him! Surely he wouldn't be mad at her any longer. He'd thank her, then they could work things out. As if to confirm her hopes, Todd looked at her with more emotion in his eyes than she'd ever seen. He seemed about to reach out to her when something in his expression changed and his whole body stiffened.

Todd's face was stony, and his coffee brown eyes looked cold and empty, making her shiver uncontrollably in the icy water. "Thanks for saving me. But from now on, Liz, I don't want to see you."

Elizabeth froze in shock. She saw Maria and Enid stiffen beside Todd. "What?"

Todd's jaw tightened. "You heard me. I don't want to see you anymore. I can't let you keep playing with me the way you have been." He closed his eyes, and when he spoke again, his voice sounded distant and harsh, not at all like Todd. "I won't play the fool anymore, Liz."

Elizabeth's heart sank. She clutched the edge of the boat, anxious to get in, to talk to Todd, to make him understand. She couldn't stand to see him so upset with her.

"Come on, Liz," Jessica yelled, maneuvering the speedboat toward her. Jessica put the engine in idle, leaned over the side of the boat, and extended her hand. Elizabeth felt dead inside, so empty she could barely make herself paddle to the speedboat. She kept staring back at Todd, hoping for some sign he'd changed his mind, some sign he didn't hate her. But he never once offered her a spark of hope. Instead his gaze seemed to grow more icy and distant as his boat drifted away. Almost in a daze, she allowed her sister to drag her inside the boat to safety.

She was suddenly tired, and cold, and weary. She ached all over, from the tips of her toes to the roots of her hair, and all the way from the inside out. Jessica grabbed a towel and wrapped it around Elizabeth's shoulders, and Elizabeth shuddered, collapsing against her.

"It's going to be OK," Jessica whispered, rubbing her hands up and down Elizabeth's arms to try and warm her. But Elizabeth shook her head, her body trembling violently. *It would never be OK again,* she thought miserably. Because she would *never, ever* forget the cold, hard, dead look in Todd's eyes.

Jessica gave her twin another hug for encouragement, grimacing at the shocked and glazed expression on Elizabeth's face. "I have to find out what Lila did to help Courtney with her scheme," she muttered. Elizabeth just sat there shaking like a leaf, looking pale and lifeless, worrying Jessica even more.

"Don't worry, Liz. Courtney and Lila won't get away with this," Jessica said. A wave of renewed anger rushed through her, and she turned her attention to the yacht. She had to get onboard. She had no idea what Lila's part in this whole thing was, but after witnessing Lila's little tête-à-tête with Devon, she had a feeling it had something to do with him. And Jessica didn't intend to let that girl get away with stealing Devon when she was just making headway herself. And look what they'd done to Todd and Elizabeth!

Suddenly she heard the roar of an engine. She and Elizabeth both jerked up their heads to see another speedboat pulling away from the yacht, with Devon in the back. Jessica opened her mouth to yell out, but then she noticed in horror that someone was with him. Lila! And she was cradled against Devon's chest. Jessica heard Elizabeth gasp.

Jessica glanced at her sister to make certain she

hadn't passed out. A minute ago she hadn't thought Elizabeth could get any paler, but her sister's skin turned completely chalky and the pupils of her eyes dilated, looking enormous in the sparse moonlight. Jessica was so upset, she bit the inside of her cheek and tasted blood.

This was too much. Lila and Devon?

Jessica's ready to kill Lila, and Elizabeth has lost both Todd and Devon. With relationships crumbling all around them, will the Sweet Valley High junior class be able to pull together to win a post-prom interschool competition? Find out in Sweet Valley High #143, **Party Weekend!,** *the third book in a fabulous, four-part prom miniseries.*

Bantam Books in the Sweet Valley High series
Ask your bookseller for the books you have missed